MW00511271

the love we vow

Victoria Everleigh

Publishing Services provided by Paper Raven Books

Printed in the United States of America

First Printing, 2022

Paperback ISBN= 978-1-7375413-0-1
Hardback ISBN= 978-1-7375413-1-8

Jason, thank you for believing in my dreams.

I love you.

Prologue

———●●———

V iolet steadied herself with the railing and trudged up the stairs toward the pulsating music on the other side of the familiar wooden door. If she knew him as well as she thought she did, he'd be here. No doubt.

The music beat louder as she neared the top. She heard the collective chatter of the crowd and the clinking glasses. Violet kicked the swinging door open with her foot.

She passed her driver's license to the grumpy-looking bouncer on a stool. Without moving his head, his eyes glanced back and forth between Violet and her ID. Without so much as a smile, he passed it back to her and nodded her in.

It'd been three months since she was last here and never had she come alone. She was always with *him*. She tugged at her top, trying to cover her full cleavage. She supposed that was to be expected in the second trimester.

She waded through a crowd of sweaty singles, some pretending and others genuinely trying to find humor in the people they were near. By contrast, she was sure her face read panic.

She rounded the first corner of the bar and started squinting to find him at his spot at the bar. Yep, there he was. Drink in hand, he threw his head back and laughed with a red-headed woman in a black dress. Violet rolled her eyes. Of course, he was smiling. He had no idea what he was about to learn. She slid through the shoulder-to-shoulder crowd to get closer. As she inched toward him, his left hand maneuvered to the woman's thigh and then up to the small of her back. He'd already moved on? Who was she?

But it didn't matter who it was because, in the next breath, he pulled the mystery woman close and started kissing her. How could he?! Tears instantly sprouted from her eyes. Instinctively, she cradled her stomach. She couldn't tell him now. Maybe not ever.

Chapter 1

———●●———

"Sadie, have you seen my phone?" Violet called from her bedroom. It was their first morning living in their Auntie Rose's fully furnished, oceanside bungalow in Ogunquit, Maine. Such were the perks of having an aunt who married a hedge fund manager. Auntie Rose and "Uncle" Petr (who liked to remind people there was only one "E" in his name) ditched Maine for Nantucket, or "Nanny Tucket," as Auntie Rose called it.

"Nope. Did you check the bathroom?" her sister, Sadie, asked. They were Irish twins, only eleven months apart. Sadie was born in January and Violet later that year in December.

Snow bunnies, they were called by family, for both their birth months and their matching blonde hair.

"I did. It's not there. I was hoping to get out of here like fifteen minutes ago, but I literally can't find it."

"Where are you going?"

Violet tore through the kitchen and scoured the counter. "Church."

"Is today a random holiday or something? Shit, did Mom call to remind us to go?" Not a holy day of obligation went by that their mother didn't send a reminder text. Sadie had no proclivities for religion or spirituality. She blew where the wind took her.

"No. Calm down," Violet answered. "I'm just going to pray. I need some peace and quiet to collect my thoughts."

"Don't tell me you're going to beg for forgiveness again. When are you going to forgive yourself and accept everything?" Sadie looked up from her incessant scrolling on her phone.

"I'm not getting into this with you," Violet said as she double-checked her hair's reflection in the microwave door and repositioned her messy bun.

"Why do you care what your hair looks like? Trying to impress the priest?" Sadie asked.

"Ha ha, very funny. Some of us care about how we present ourselves to the world, regardless of whether we're going to run into any hot guys. Plus, most priests are older than Grandpa." Violet shuffled some papers around on the kitchen table, hoping her phone would materialize.

"Hmm, well in that case, if you married one of them, he'd be dead soon, and you'd inherit some money."

"You're ridiculous. Catholic priests don't get married, and they take a vow of poverty. Stop fantasizing about a religious sugar daddy."

"It's working for Auntie Rose."

Violet laughed. "True, but Petr isn't religious."

"Remember, it's *Uncle* Petr to you."

"Right."

Violet paused, put her hands on her hips, and declared that she might just leave without her phone. "Come find me in thirty minutes if I'm not back." She yanked open the fridge and grabbed a bottle of water. "Found it!" She snatched her chilled iPhone from the top shelf.

"In the fridge?" Sadie asked.

"Yea, I'm not sure how it got there." She waved her hand. "Don't pretend you haven't done it before.

Sadie chuckled. "True. Have fun." As Violet left the house, she blew her older sister a kiss.

The map showed a five-minute walk to the All Saints Catholic Church. She and Sadie hadn't so much as stepped foot in their Aunt's bungalow before signing on the proverbial dotted line. It was a leap of faith, so to speak, and Violet was happy when she'd discovered a Catholic Church nearby.

Violet paused outside the small, white-brick chapel nestled among the neighborhood homes. A sign outside advertised the summer worship schedule: Mass on Saturday nights and Sunday mornings and afternoons. Confessions were one half hour before Mass and on Monday afternoons.

Despite being delayed by her missing iPhone, she was right on time, but half-wished that she had arrived too late to go to confession.

As she pulled the black knob on the massive door, the familiar, smoky scent of incense hit her. It was cool, still, and a little dark inside. She closed her eyes and inhaled, then slowly walked toward the confessional. A bright red light above the confessional booth indicated that it was occupied. As Violet got closer, though, she paused and then turned away quickly. She would come back…later. *Then again, it's not going to get any easier, so I might as well do it now with a priest who hasn't already heard my sins over and over.* She pivoted again and walked to the back of the church. Her mind raced with opposing thoughts—leave or stay? *No, not today. Not today. I'll do this next week.* She knelt before entering the last row of pews and made the sign of the cross while facing the altar, "In the name of the Father, and of the Son, and of the Holy Spirit. Amen." The red light above the confessional clicked off, and Violet lifted her head to see an older woman walk out, stringing through her Rosary beads.

Violet shifted in her pew, trying to avoid eye contact, but in a chapel so small, one couldn't really hide. The priest knelt in front of the altar and made the sign of the cross before proceeding down the aisle toward the back of the church.

He looked friendly, but Violet just wanted to be alone. She could escape a possible conversation if she just closed her eyes and pretended to be deep in prayer, but was the priest like the Sin Whisperer, able to detect anyone's sin just by looking at them? As Violet's eyes opened, she realized he was looking right at her.

"Welcome. I'm Father Goren."

"Nice to meet you. I'm Violet."

"Is this your first time here?" Father Goren asked.

"It is," she said. "My sister and I just moved here from Boston."

"Very nice. I went to seminary in Boston. Great city, but I have a soft spot for Ogunquit. What brought you and your sister here?"

She considered sharing her whole life's saga but opted for the simpler answer. "I'm going to be a reporter at Portland's ABC station, and my sister is getting her master's in music composition at the University of Southern Maine."

"That's lovely. Please, tell your sister if she ever wants to lend us her musical gifts, we would be more than blessed."

Violet laughed. "She's not really a church-going person, but I'll mention it to her."

"I understand. Violet, it was a pleasure to meet you. I hope to see you again. If you come to Mass this weekend, please be sure to say hi afterward."

Chapter 2

Tristan vigorously swished the spearmint wash in his mouth, making sure to hit every corner for exactly sixty seconds. He combed his hair back with a hint of gel and applied his Tom's Mountain Spring deodorant. He couldn't live in southern Maine and not use Tom's of Maine products.

The wall clock read 4:50 a.m. He picked up his bag and stepped out into the crisp, pre-dawn air. Tristan craved quiet mornings like this, just him and God on a walk to the gym.

"Good morning, Father," Mindy welcomed him from the Quest Fitness front desk.

"Nice to see you." He hoped she wouldn't launch into a long conversation about her grandchildren when all he wanted was to work out.

"That was a beautiful homily you said this weekend," she said. "Just precious."

Mindy gave a similar sentiment every Thursday morning. Tristan figured that he could speak gibberish on Sunday, and she'd still think it was perfect. He knew he should appreciate her compliments, but at this hour, he didn't want to talk to anyone. That's why he came to the gym before the sun rose. He'd be less likely to run into any parishioners and explain, yet again, that yes, priests do in fact exercise.

"Thank you, Mrs. Medina."

"I know I'm old enough to be your mother, but please, call me Mindy, and don't let me tell you again." Again, this was another one of her weekly barbs.

"Yes ma'am."

"You enjoy your workout, Father."

"Will I see you at the noon Mass?" Tristan asked, immediately regretting continuing the conversation when he knew he had limited time at the gym.

"I wouldn't miss it."

Father Tristan walked into the empty locker room and put his bag in his locker, which the staff affectionately labeled with a "Padre" magnet. He didn't speak Spanish, but the gym's manager said he reminded her of her parish priest back home in Colombia. She, like most older women in town, doted on Father Tristan. He knew he was attractive—everyone always told him so. He had excellent listening skills and a white collar; in other words, he was an old lady chick magnet.

He opened a tub of Clorox wipes and started his routine of wiping down both the outside and inside of his locker. He had four Apple Pie Larabars perfectly stacked on the top shelf, in case he ever forgot a snack, which he never had. In the back of the locker, a Bible quote hung: "For while bodily training is of some value, godliness is of value in every way, as it holds promise for the present life and also for the life to come" (1 Timothy 4:8). His spiritual director recommended he see it each morning as a reminder of what's truly important.

As he threw his car keys into his bag, his phone started to vibrate. He retrieved it and saw a text from the parish secretary. He rolled his eyes and grunted. What could be so important this early in the morning?

"Please call me when you get a chance. Re: Father Goren."

He threw his phone back in his bag and headed onto the gym floor. It wasn't like the parish secretary to text so early in the morning. *Damn it. Why did I sacrifice my twenty minutes of solace by checking my phone before my gym time?*

Once on the gym floor, he jumped onto an elliptical, placing himself in the back row of the machines. He usually kept his head down, not wanting to catch the eye of anyone. Sometimes, he felt like being a priest meant he always had to be "on" and be ready to listen to anyone who wanted to talk. His spiritual director reminded him that even Jesus needed rest and time away from his flock.

He usually strode in silence, but today, he turned to the local news station on the mini TV built into the elliptical and turned up the volume. The weather report was the only segment he actually tuned into, especially with a potential tropical storm brewing. The ominous gray clouds that accompanied him on his walk to the gym didn't bode well. He hoped to beat the rain on his way back to the rectory. On the TV, the camera jumped to a young reporter struggling to stay upright on the beach as her hair blew violently in the wind. He squinted and looked closer.

Violet?

As soon as he asked, her name popped up on the bottom of the screen.

Violet Marie. *Marie* was her middle name. She told him once that she preferred not to use her last name on TV.

He slowed his pace on the elliptical to steady his view and enabled the audio to hear her voice. How could this be happening? And after all this time? He assumed Violet was new in town because he'd never noticed her on the morning news before. There was no way that he would have missed her if she had been on air before. But he couldn't pay attention to what she said about the impending tropical storm, lightning, thunder, or rain.

Why God? Why would you bring her so close to me?

He shook his head and changed the channel. He returned to a faster pace on the elliptical. He thought of his hero, Saint Pope John Paul II, who said, "In the designs of Providence, there are no mere coincidences." This couldn't be a coincidence. He wanted to deny the thrill of seeing her or the chance they might run into each other. Was it bad to look forward to the possibility?

He contemplated just giving up, getting off the elliptical, showering, and forgetting about what he saw. What did it change, really? So, she lived in the area. Big deal. Portland had a lot of suburbs. What are the odds that they even live near each other? If he wanted to know, how would he find out anyway? Plus, he assumed she was dating someone. Heck, she might even be married.

He wished he'd looked a little closer to see if she wore a ring. The thought of her being married calmed him. It would mean they both were in permanent states in life. It would mean both had made lasting choices. Case closed.

Did Violet know he was a priest now? It wouldn't surprise him if she didn't. He had kept a low profile when he joined the seminary six and a half years ago. He'd deleted all of his social media accounts and kept in touch with only a few close friends. Many hadn't understood why he chose to become a priest, but there were still a supportive few. He had to admit that it was definitely out of character for how his life had been up until that point.

He didn't want to think about his past, Violet, or their break-up. He'd said his final vows as a priest. This was the life he was called to, but he couldn't understand why Violet would reappear if not for some bigger reason. Had she orchestrated the move to be closer to him? He quickly laughed the idea off, reminding himself to be humble.

He tried to talk to himself as his spiritual director would, encouraging him to live in the moment more, be present with God, and not analyze so much. But this was too much. He sped up on the elliptical, striding with urgency and hoping to forget about Violet.

Chapter 3

Violet stood over the stove at Jude's apartment, stirring the chicken noodle soup. She heard her grandma's voice in her head saying, "A watched pot never boils." Just over a year of long-distance dating was enough for both of them. With Jude living in Wells, they were only ten minutes apart. Now, if he could just hurry up and propose, Violet would appreciate it very much, thank you. Her thirtieth birthday was just about a year past, and she found that people's sympathy for one's thirty-first birthday paled in comparison to the sympathy they showered over one's thirtieth. Plus, she knew her limited supply of eggs dwindled every twenty-eight days.

"You're the best, Vi," Jude said from the couch, his broad shoulders and long legs hidden under a heap of blankets and quilts with his toes peeking out at the bottom. It was day four of bronchitis, and his cough still sounded violent.

"I try," she teased with a flip of her hair.

"I was going to ask if you could put some of those mini Saltines on the side."

"You got it! I know it hurts when you talk, but your voice sounds sexy when it's raspy."

Jude coughed. "Are you hitting on me in a vulnerable state?"

"Maybe. Do you need some more water?"

"Yes, that would be great," he said, lifting his glass in Violet's direction. "Ok, so how many words does your bio need to be for the website?"

"About two hundred. You know I hate writing about myself, so just throw something together. My boss wants it tomorrow." Tomorrow as in 3:00 a.m., as in the morning shift, before the sun rises.

She refilled his glass with water from a pitcher. "You should drink this entire glass, plus eat all of the soup. You need lots of fluids."

"Thank you, nurse." Jude took his first slurp of salty chicken noodle soup. "Ok, so how about this? 'Violet Marie is the latest and greatest member of Portland ABC's morning news team. Not only is she gorgeous, but she's also smart and kind. She makes a mean chocolate cupcake, which is only rivaled by her gingerbread pancakes. Don't get too attached to her in the mornings because she'll soon be gracing your TVs in primetime.'"

Violet laughed. "That's a no. It needs to be formal, like, 'Violet Marie recently joined the Portland ABC news team after eight years as a reporter in the New England area.' Yada, yada, you get the idea."

"So basically, it should be all facts and no flavor?"

Violet shrugged. "Yea, that's a good way of putting it."

"Ok, so let's say we start with that sentence you said and then launch into something boring like, 'She graduated from Merrimack College with a degree in journalism. She served as a morning show reporter in Springfield, MA before joining the team in Boston for six years. She's excited to call the Pine Tree State home now.'"

Violet wriggled her nose. "Is that what Maine is known as?"

"Yep."

"I guess I should know that. I thought it was the Lighthouse State or something like that."

"This is really good soup by the way, and excellent crackers."

"You can thank Campbell's," Violet smirked. "You'll just have to make it up to me when you're all better."

"Varano's?"

"Yes!" Violet exclaimed, salivating at the thought of the Italian restaurant's crispy chicken parmesan and warm bread basket. She remembered their second date over such a meal just over a year ago.

"Do you feel well enough to show your open houses tomorrow?" Violet asked.

"Not right now, but my dad said he'd take care of them if I can't."

"Your dad? When was the last time he did an open house?"

"It's been a while, but he's the only person the sellers are comfortable with if I can't."

"They sound picky."

"They definitely are, and they're very demanding, too," Jude said. "But I think their house will sell quickly, and we won't have to deal with them for too long."

"Did they already find another house?"

"No. They decided to move into one of the homes they already own."

"It must be nice to decide which home to live in on any given day," Violet lamented.

The doorbell buzzed. "Who's that?" Jude asked.

"I don't know. Don't act all innocent. Is there another girl you forgot to tell me about?" Violet laughed.

"Yes, of course! I planned it that way. I wanted you two to meet," he joked. "But really, I'm not expecting anybody. Do you mind buzzing them in?"

Violet got up and pinged for the visitor.

"Seacoast Pizza," a male voice boomed.

"You sneak! You ordered pizza!" Jude feigned a scandalous tone.

"Guilty!" Violet giggled. "I'm sorry. I really didn't want to eat soup."

"That makes two of us," Jude confessed.

"You said you liked it!" Violet lightly punched Jude in the shoulder.

"I did, but I just said that to make you happy. The only reason I'm still eating it is that it feels good on my throat."

The pizza delivery guy knocked at the door. "Give him twenty for the tip," Jude said.

"Are you sure? That's more than the entire pizza costs."

"I'm positive. My wallet is right there," Jude pointed.

Violet fished two twenty-dollar bills from his wallet. She opened the door and exchanged the bills for the pizza, excited to see the delivery boy's reaction to the generous tip. Jude's generosity was one of the many characteristics Violet loved about him. He always acknowledged "the little guy" and appreciated people who performed menial tasks, like delivering pizza, scrubbing floors, or bagging groceries.

"What kind d'you get?" Jude asked.

"Mmm, your favorite." She pulled a slice of pepperoni out of the box. "It smells so good! I could just stick my nose in there."

"Are you going to share?"

"Maybe. But you have to promise that you'll finish the soup and this extra glass of water. I can't trust you to drink your fluids when I'm not around." She pulled another plate out of the cabinet and plopped a piece of the thick-crust pizza on it. They sat in silence for a few minutes while they ate.

"I wish you could join me on the couch."

Violet frowned. "Me too, but I don't want to get sick during my first week on the job."

"I know. I'm just teasing. It's just hard to see you sitting across the room and not be able to kiss you."

Violet blew him a kiss.

"Not the same thing," Jude frowned.

"It's nice not to worry about one of us driving two hours back home at night anymore, though." Violet eyed the clock. She'd have to leave soon if she wanted to get at least six hours of sleep, but would one less hour of sleep really make a difference? "So, I went to All Saints the other day. Have you been there?"

"Of course."

"It was really quaint. I wasn't in there that long. I met the priest, who was nice." *And I successfully avoided going to confession.*

"Father Goren, right?"

"Yea!"

"He was one of my teachers at Saint James School," Jude explained. "Everyone loves him."

"I can see why. I can walk to the church from our place, so I think I'll go to Mass until it closes for the season. Then I'll join you at Saint Mary's. Do you want to come with me on Sunday?"

Tristan croaked up a hearty cough. "Totally, as long as I'm feeling better. It would be nice to see Father Goren. I doubt he remembers me, though."

"But you're unforgettable..." she cooed.

"I didn't exactly stand out growing up," he said. "I wasn't the goody two-shoes, but I also wasn't the rebel. My social status was somewhere in the middle, so I'm sure I fell by the wayside."

"If I'd met you back then, I wouldn't have forgotten about you." She stared intently into Jude's eyes, not blinking. She and Jude broke into laughter together.

"Can you grab me another?" Jude offered up his plate. She served each of them another slice of pizza, along with a fistful of napkins to mop up all the grease.

"It's still crazy to me that your parents sent you to Catholic school when they were atheists, and then all these years later, they converted to Catholicism." Violet settled back on to the reclining chair across from the couch.

"Yea, I don't know why it happened that way, either."

"I'm grateful it did."

"What time do you want to go to Mass on Sunday?" he asked.

"It'll have to be the noon Mass because I'm not done with work until 11 a.m."

"Noon, it is," Jude said. "It's too bad All Saints isn't open year round. There are enough people to sustain it."

Violet sighed. "It's a bummer. I bet Father Goren is needed at other parishes with the priest shortage."

Jude took the last bite of his crust. "On that note, I'm going to kick you out because I know you'll hate yourself—and me—tomorrow morning when you wake up."

"To call that hour 'morning' is generous," Violet joked.

"What time does your alarm go off?"

"Ugh, too early! 1:30 a.m." Violet dragged herself off the couch. "I'm taking the pizza for breakfast tomorrow."

"Cold pizza is the best," Jude agreed.

"We see eye to eye on this stuff. This is why we're in love," Violet teased and blew him a kiss. "Email me the finished bio!"

Chapter 4

Violet wrangled her grandma's old Rosary out of her purse and started sliding each bead through her fingers as she waited in line outside the confessional. She could almost smell her grandma when she brought the beads close to her face. Her grandma had been her biggest cheerleader, always ready with a kiss and a hug. Anytime you needed her, she'd have a teapot on the stove and two pink, faded mugs that either said, "Best Grandma Ever" or "TGIF: This Grandma is Fabulous." As her mint tea steeped in the mug and the milk transformed the dark liquid to something more caramel in color, she'd do a combination of listening, laughing, and storytelling. She'd insert a validating look of concern, or say "That's tough," or squeeze her hand. How Violet longed for that right now. She especially found solace in her grandma's hugs, a warmth and comfort that surpassed even her own mother's touch. *Miss you, Grandma.*

The man in front of her in line at confession kept shifting his weight from side to side. Violet wondered what his sins were. Lust? Adultery? She noticed his wedding band and wondered where his kids and wife were. *Maybe he just wanted an excuse to get out of the house for some quiet.* She caught herself silently chastising him for wearing a New England Patriots hoodie and shorts to church but then chided herself on such a quick judgement.

It was a nice distraction to think about other people's sins. Another woman got in line behind Violet, and they exchanged small smiles with a "yea, me too" look shared amongst those waiting for confession.

Sure, they pretended not to judge, but Violet couldn't help but wonder whether anyone else's sins were as egregious as hers. *What would these people think if they knew what I've done?*

The green light turned on above the confessional as a nun walked out, signaling that the next person could enter. Violet always laughed to herself when she saw nuns at confession. *What could they possibly have to confess?* You never wanted to go into confession after a nun because it always made your sins sound worse comparatively. She was relieved that Man in the Patriots Sweatshirt would be first to go after the nun.

Violet kept shifting her weight back and forth, gripping the Rosary beads. Man in the Patriots Sweatshirt emerged not long thereafter and found his way to a pew. This was it. Her turn. Violet contemplated just crawling into the confessional at this point. She kept her death grip on the beads as she parted the curtain and knelt down.

"Forgive me, Father, for I have sinned. It has been about a month since my last confession." Violet slowly shut her eyes. "In that time, there's been a lot, as usual." She continued with a laundry list of venial sins and paused with a big sigh. "I also haven't been completely honest with someone about something that they deserve to know. It happened so long ago, but it's eating at me. Maybe it's not a sin. I don't know." She rubbed her sweaty palms against her black dress pants.

Father Goren cleared his throat. Violet was unsure if he wanted more information or just had a tickle in his throat. "So you're concerned that by not telling this person a particular piece of information that you've sinned?"

"Exactly."

"Without knowing exactly what happened, I can't make a specific suggestion, but if this person knew the information you have, would it change his or her life?"

"Probably."

"I'm not saying that should be the basis for whether you tell this person. I'm trying to understand the gravity of the situation."

"It has to do with a mistake I made," Violet explained. "It was probably the biggest mistake of my life, and I confessed that years ago. Since then, though, I've wondered if I also need to confess that I kept this mistake a secret from a certain person."

"I see," Father Goren said.

They fell into a short silence. "May I make a suggestion?"

"Yes, please, Father."

"You may want to consider spending an hour in silence with Our Lord at Adoration and talk to him about this situation that troubles you. When you're in the presence of Our Lord, see which path brings you more peace. There are many churches in the area that offer Adoration weekly."

Violet smiled. "I like that idea."

She considered divulging more of her past. Did Father Goren *need* to know? She learned that sometimes the details weren't as important to the priest as the desire to repent and bask in God's mercy.

"For your penance, three Hail Marys and one Our Father. Now, please say an Act of Contrition," he said. "You can find a copy of it in the pamphlet."

Violet reached for the prayer card. How did she not have the Act of Contrition memorized by this point? *It's not like I haven't been to confession enough times.*

"In the name of the Father, and of the Son, and of the Holy Spirit. Amen," she said as she made the sign of the cross. "My God, I am sorry for my sins with all my heart. In choosing to do wrong and failing to do good, I have sinned against you, whom I should love above all things. I firmly intend, with your help, to do penance, to sin no more, and to avoid whatever leads me to sin. Our Savior Jesus Christ suffered and died for us. In his name, my God, have mercy."

"God, the Father of mercies, through the death and the resurrection of his Son has reconciled the world to himself and sent the Holy Spirit among us for the forgiveness of sins; through the ministry of the Church, may God give you pardon and peace, and I absolve you from your sins in the name of the Father, and of the Son, and of the Holy Spirit," Father Goren replied. "God has freed you from your sin. You may go in peace."

"Amen. Thank you, Father."

She knew Father Goren couldn't tell her what to do and that confession wasn't supposed to serve as therapy, but despite being absolved of her sin of concealing information, she wondered whether God's mercy would ever extinguish that gnawing feeling in her stomach.

She picked a pew toward the back of the church and knelt down.

"Hail Mary, full of Grace, the Lord is with thee. Blessed art thou among women and blessed is the fruit of thy womb Jesus. Holy Mary, Mother of God, pray for us sinners now and at the hour of our death. Amen." Violet repeated it two more times and finished with the Our Father, as the Rosary beads ran through her fingers, appreciating their cool touch against her sweaty hands.

She pulled out her phone. Jude texted that he'd arrive in about five minutes. Violet quietly set the kneeler back in its place and nestled into the pew, her hands folded in her lap as she relished the near silence of the church. She overheard a few "Good morning" and "How are you?" greetings.

She closed her eyes, voyaging back to earlier days when her grandma and mom carted her and Sadie to Mass, usually in matching dresses and shoes. They'd get so excited to attend the kids' Mass, which was held in a glass room right next to the altar. Their mom loved how they held hands walking to the front of the church, where they'd congregate with the other children and then be led away to "the kids' room." It comforted Violet, who usually sat perched in the glass window, that she could always see her mom and grandma. She had looked forward to the day when she'd get to sit, stand, and kneel at the same time and in the same area as the adults. Sometimes, she'd just imitate what they did, instead of listening to the room chaperone, who read Bible stories. Sadie, meanwhile, whispered in the corner with a tribe of willing participants. Even then, Sadie rebelled against Mass.

Violet smiled to herself, thinking of those simpler days. She wondered what happened in the ensuing years that took her so far away from that innocent, little girl peering in the church window.

Jude interrupted her thoughts by sliding into the pew next to her. He knelt down to pray briefly. She squeezed his hand and let go, wanting to savor the silence before Mass.

Thank God Jude knows everything already.

The organ bellowed, and Mass started. It hit her during Mass that all Sundays would be like this: Mass with Jude close by and no more alternating weekends in each other's cities.

After receiving Communion, Violet knelt down to pray. This was her favorite part. She closed her eyes and mentally recited the name of every person she loved, asking God to keep them safe and healthy this week. At one point, she glanced over at Jude, and her stomach dropped. How could she potentially promise her life to one man while harboring a secret from another, a past lover, who deserved to know?

She grinned, thinking about how, if Sadie were here, she'd tell her that her thoughts were spiraling. "What if, what if, what if…" Sadie would say. "Let's stop what-if-ing and start living."

At the end of Mass, Father Goren made a couple of announcements about an upcoming Bible study and a food drive the church would host that week. "Finally, I'd like to thank you all for your support during this very difficult week. You may have heard that my sister suffered a stroke a few days ago and is currently in hospice care."

There were a few audible gasps throughout the church.

"I will be traveling down to be beside her in Rhode Island for the next two weeks. But don't worry. You will be in good hands with Deacon Joe, as well as two visiting priests from Kennebunk, who will share duties in my absence."

Father Goren closed in prayer.

"That's so sad about his sister," Violet said as she and Jude walked out of the church. Father Goren stood outside, greeting all of the congregants.

"My girlfriend, Violet, and I are praying for your sister and your family," Jude said, shaking hands with Father Goren. Violet wondered when her title would be changed to fiancée.

"Thank you so much," Father Goren said. "Violet, it's so nice to see you again. I'm glad you decided to join us." Had he connected the dots, realizing it was her in the confessional earlier?

"Me too," she replied. "Jude actually went to Saint James School growing up, about twenty-five years ago."

"Is that right?" Father Goren asked, his eyebrows raised.

"Yea, I live in Wells now and go to Saint Mary's."

"That's lovely. The two of you are always welcome here."

"Thank you." Violet and Jude walked away, not wanting to monopolize Father Goren's time when so many other people waited to wish him well.

"See, I told you he didn't remember me," Jude said.

Violet shrugged. "You're right. You were forgettable, I guess."

Jude tickled her gently in the crease of her elbow, and she squirmed with a giggle. "Want to go to brunch?"

"You know it."

She thought that moving to Maine would give her the distance she needed from everything that had happened, but instead, she was just as wracked with guilt. Would this follow her wherever she went?

"Vi, you ok?"

She took a deep breath. "I thought I'd feel differently here, you know. I thought this would be a fresh start, but I still feel so guilty for having never told Tristan about the twins. No matter how often I go to confession, I'm undecided about what to do."

Jude rubbed her back as they walked along the sidewalk. "You know I'll support you in whatever you decide. I wish I could take this burden off of you."

"Would you want to know? If you were Tristan?"

Jude seemed to think about it with a long inhale. "Yea, I would want to know if I were in his position." He squeezed Violet's hand. At their two-month anniversary, Jude had opened up about his ex-girlfriend, Leona, who had also been pregnant, but the difference was that she told Jude right away. When Leona miscarried, they had grieved together. His experience made her feel accepted and understood by him in a way that few could.

She groaned. "I figured you would say that. I don't even know how I would contact him anyway."

They stopped at a crosswalk as cars drove by them. "You're a journalist. Out of anyone, you could figure out what he's up to or where he lives."

"But it also means I have no excuse not to find him if I wanted to." They continued down the street, waving in thanks to the car that had stopped for them to cross.

"It seems like the indecision has really been weighing on you lately," Jude probed.

"Woodrow Wilson said, 'No man can rationally live, worship, or love his neighbor on an empty stomach.' Therefore, I'll at least wait until after brunch to decide." *And then I'll probably still be undecided.*

Jude laughed. "I've never heard that one before, but I'll take your word for it."

Chapter 5

Tristan couldn't get Violet out of his head as he drove down I-95 to Ogunquit for weekend Mass. He laughed at himself for thinking that he could. It was like that silly pink elephant. Don't think about a pink elephant. You're thinking about a pink elephant.

His first Mass would be the Saturday evening vigil. Then, Father Joe would take the services on Sunday at 7:30 and 9 a.m., and Tristan would celebrate the last Mass at noon. Father Joe was probably the only priest Tristan could trade barbs with over who celebrates the morning Masses. Both men loved the crack of dawn.

He was proud of himself for not Googling Violet's name after seeing her on TV at the gym. If he just stayed off the Internet and stopped watching the local ABC station, then he'd be fine. He could pretend she didn't live in the area or even exist at all. That would solve his curiosity. He hoped.

Tristan rarely ventured down to Ogunquit because the church was only open during the summer, the tourist season, and Father Goren rarely asked for coverage. He arrived at the rectory about an hour before he needed to hear confessions.

He liked to acquaint himself with a church by sitting in the pews in silence and taking in the church's distinct scent. He always made a point to stop by the candles that parishioners lit with their intentions: the healing of a spouse, the passing of an exam, or getting a promotion at work. The candles represented their hope for a positive outcome or a better future. Often, it brought him hope to see so many others' faith in those flickering lights.

Only a few people came for confession that afternoon. It was the end of summer, so the tourist season was slowing down. Plus, a tropical storm was due the next day and the winds were picking up, which usually meant even fewer people came to Mass.

Father Goren said there'd be no music for the Saturday Mass because their organist had returned to college for the year. The lack of music easily cut out fifteen minutes from Mass. Before Tristan became a priest, he referred to such services as "microwave Masses." They were his favorite because he could check "Mass" off the to-do list, look like a devoted Catholic, and feel good about himself. He laughed at life's sense of humor now that he was a priest who preached to people who also undoubtedly hoped Mass would fly by.

Tristan liked to greet the parishioners on their way out of the church. He didn't know everyone, but he had pride in being their shepherd, so to speak. It was fun to change locations and see some new faces.

"Have a beautiful weekend, and stay safe!" he said more than a few times.

What if one of these people had a connection to Violet? He shook his head and assured himself that it would mean nothing anyway.

* * * * *

Thirty minutes before the noon Mass on Sunday, Violet pushed the maroon drape to the right and stepped into the wooden confessional. She lowered herself onto the cushioned kneeler, a golden lattice and black screen hiding her from the priest on the other side.

"Forgive me, Father, for I have sinned," she said. "It has been…one week since my last confession." She sighed, her head bowed.

"May the Lord be in your heart and help you to confess your sins with true sorrow," the priest replied.

Violet cocked her head to make sure she heard his voice correctly. It sounded like *him*, but how could that be? She cleared her throat, coughing into her elbow, to buy time.

That voice, though. It had to be his. She needed to hear it again to be sure. If it was truly him on the other side, she didn't want him to have the same revelation about her identity. She took another deep breath.

"Are you alright?" the priest asked. "Violet?"

Violet's heart dropped like the Tower of Terror. This wasn't possible. There was no way. There had to be a camera somewhere in this confessional filming this sick joke.

"I recognized your voice," he said.

She contemplated fleeing the confessional. Surely, he wouldn't run after her. How would that look to parishioners? She could see the headline: *Young, attractive priest bolts from confessional after young woman in distress.* If Tristan was anything like he had been seven years ago, then he cared very much what people thought. So, for Violet, leaving the confessional and not returning to church until Father Goren returned seemed like the best idea.

She could barely eke out a sentence. "I don't..." She coughed. "Tristan? Are you a priest now?"

"Indeed. I'm filling in for Father Goren."

Violet mouthed to herself, "What the—" before remembering her place in a house of God.

"This is awkward."

He chuckled. "I agree. You don't have to do anything you're not comfortable with." *Comfortable?* Since when did Tristan care about Violet being comfortable?

"I think I'll pass." She rose from the kneeler and pushed the curtain to the side. She kept her head bowed, averting her gaze from the people waiting in line.

Once she was in the vestibule, she fled out the door and started running. The rain was spitting now. Even though she'd reported on the impending storm, she forgot to bring an umbrella. She just wanted to get home. She knew she'd find Sadie there, and the two of them could drown her sorrows in a pint of mint chocolate chip ice cream. Her pace quickened as she saw the house on the horizon.

"What are you doing back so early?" Sadie asked as Violet slammed the front door behind her.

"You'll seriously never guess who I just saw at church." Violet threw her soggy sweater onto the floor and ran into the bedroom to change into some dry clothes.

"Not in the mood to play. Just tell me."

"Tristan."

"At church?"

"Actually, let me correct myself," Violet yelled from her bedroom. "He's Father Tristan now."

"What? We need wine."

Violet returned to their tiny living room in a pair of joggers and a University of Southern Maine hoodie. Sadie grabbed a bottle of Malbec from their wine rack, opened it, and poured a healthy serving into two stemless glasses. "Sit and drink. Normally, I'd bitch to you about stealing my clothes, but I won't."

"Thank you," Violet replied, relieved, as Sadie passed her a glass.

"Ok, out with it." Sadie settled into the couch.

Violet plopped down, cradled a pink, tufted pillow to her chest, and described the two-minute exchange. One moment, she felt like her life was going well, and the next, her entire past flashed before her eyes.

"And he thought you might still want to make a confession? What an arrogant piece of shit!"

Violet shook her head.

Sadie acted more riled up than she was. "I'm still not comprehending the fact that Tristan is a priest. A priest? Don't they have to abstain from sex their whole lives?"

"They're supposed to while they're a priest."

"He's the last person I'd ever imagine to sign up for that," Sadie exclaimed. "I'm stunned. I kind of want to go over there and see for myself."

Violet shrugged. "I honestly don't even care if you do that. He deserves to feel uneasy."

"He always knew I didn't like him," Sadie said. "It's because I could see right through his little charade as the good guy. He was a snake."

"He was emotionally unavailable."

"Yea, that was your therapist's nice way of saying that he was an asshole."

"Well, I think calling him a snake is a little harsh," Violet said.

"Oh my gosh! You're defending him!"

"No, I'm not." Violet took a long gulp of her wine.

"Remember that I'm on your team, Violet. Tristan—or *Father* Tristan—wasn't there for you in your worst moments."

"Yea, but that's because he didn't *know*."

Sadie rolled her eyes. "I'm glad to see your defense of him is as strong as ever."

Violet threw her pillow onto the floor. "No. All I'm saying is that I wasn't exactly an innocent party in all of this. I didn't stand up to him. I let him walk all over me." Violet took another generous swig of Malbec. "None of it matters anyway. I think he's only here this weekend, thankfully."

"And then he goes back where?"

"No clue," Violet answered.

"I'm going to Google him."

"Please don't."

"Well, I still will, but I won't tell you what I find."

"No, because then I'm going to want to know." Violet slammed her glass onto the coffee table, the remaining wine swishing to the edge. "Ugh! I wish I didn't care, but now I'm curious."

Sadie grabbed her laptop from the side table, sat back down, and started typing. She squinted at the screen. "Do you want me to tell you?"

Violet groaned and picked up her glass again. Why couldn't she just be apathetic about Tristan? "Yes. Tell me."

"Ok, so he's a priest at Saint Anthony's in Kennebunk. That's about thirty minutes away. It looks like he's been there for about a year."

Violet rolled her eyes and finished off her wine, reminding herself that alcohol was partly what had gotten her to this place of regret. "I hoped he was visiting from Alaska or Timbuktu."

"It doesn't look like he's on Instagram or Twitter."

"Yea, he's always been skeptical of social media, so that doesn't surprise me." Violet stood from the couch, walked into the kitchen, and opened the freezer, surveying it for dessert.

"Sorry, I finished the mint chocolate chip this morning," Sadie said.

Violet grabbed a chocolate ice cream bar, poured herself another goblet of wine, and grabbed an open bag of chips, balancing it on top of her wine glass so she only had to make one trip back to the couch.

"That's an interesting combination." Sadie grinned.

"Desperate times."

"Aren't you the one who says emotional eating isn't a coping technique?" Sadie prodded.

Violet waved her off, chomping on potato chips.

"Realistically, though, Tristan is going to return to his parish, and you'll never have to cross paths with him if you don't want to…. And you don't want to, right?"

"What kind of question is that, Sadie? Of course I don't want to see him again."

"I just didn't know if you were having second thoughts about the way things ended."

"No, definitely not," Violet said. "I haven't talked to him since we broke up. That's the way I wanted it."

"Ok, that's fine. The way you were talking a minute ago made me think you saw some bizarre redeeming quality in him."

"No. Even if he wasn't a priest, I still wouldn't want to be with him. There's literally nothing left that we share. Nothing." *But did he have a right to know?* Her stomach lurched at the thought of telling him. *Was this God's way of opening the door to tell him everything?*

"Very true," Sadie said. "Plus, Jude is way better."

"Much better. Cheers to that." Violet clinked glasses with Sadie. "Thank God I met a real man." She stood and left her second empty wine glass on the counter. "Alright, I'm going to take a nap and hopefully forget this whole ordeal."

"Try not to have a nightmare about Tristan."

Violet rolled her eyes. "Excellent advice, Sadie. I can always count on you for your wisdom."

She plopped onto her bed and wiggled underneath her comforter. Now that Tristan knew she was in the area, maybe he'd Google her. Maybe he'd figure out that she was a reporter, and maybe he'd even watch her on TV. It made her feel more self-conscious, hating that she still hoped he found her attractive. She shook her head, wanting to wring the thought from her mind.

She opened a new Internet tab on her phone and started typing into the all-knowing Google: *Should I tell my ex I was pregnant with his twins?* She closed her eyes after pressing search and threw her phone to the side. She wasn't sure she wanted to see the answers. But yes, she did. Then, she could put this pesky issue of whether to tell him to rest and get some sleep.

The Google search yielded mixed results. One old Dr. Gabby column featured a question from a reader named Elizabeth, who seemed to be in the same position as Violet. Dr. Gabby's advice was to let the past be in the past and not bring it up unless she wanted her ex-lover to be a part of her life. On another advice site, the relationship expert said it was good karma to tell the would-have-been father. But then, she didn't really believe in karma.

Violet rolled her eyes. Of course, there was no consensus on this issue.

Chapter 6

Violet settled into a pew at All Saints. She relished the last few days of the summer season that she'd be able to visit after her morning shift, finding refuge the moment the cool blast surrounded her when she entered the church. The musky incense evoked a feeling of coziness and home.

She sat for a few minutes with her back against the bench seat. It reminded her of all the times her mom insisted on arriving at church twenty minutes early to sit silently in the pews. She and Sadie dragged their feet and protested, pretending not to find their coats or shoes, demanding to know why they had to be *that* early. Now she understood. When else was there this kind of silence in daily life? When else could one contemplate uninterrupted?

She saw a few people walk in and light candles as an offering. Some people took a quick seat in the pew, said a prayer, and left within thirty seconds. She assumed it was the lunch crowd, and she smiled to herself, knowing her mom was probably doing the same right now during her break from the hospital.

Violet lowered herself onto the kneeler and made the sign of the cross. She rested her elbows on the back of the pew in front of her and rested her forehead on her hands. Another set of footsteps sounded against the tiled floor. This person obviously knew their way around the church. The footsteps grew closer and stopped beside her.

"Violet?"

Her stomach lurched. Tristan, of course. Correction: Father Tristan.

Violet opened her eyes and looked up, her heart racing. She hadn't seen his face since their break-up. He was still handsome with his jet-black hair and built frame, as though he'd never skipped a day at the gym or overindulged on ice cream. She wished he didn't look *this* good. Why was it so much harder to give men a hard time when they were attractive? Would he notice she was blushing or that her hands were clammy?

"Hi." She tempered her curiosity.

"May I?" He pointed to the pew in front of her.

She nodded.

"I'm sorry to intrude. I didn't know you were here today. I was just passing through."

Her body tensed. She tried to slow her breathing. "Was there a reason, then, that you interrupted my prayer time?" The moment she said it, she knew it came off frosty. But she didn't want him to think she was intrigued by his presence.

"I felt bad about the way our conversation ended in the confessional the other day. I had no plans to reach out to you, but when I saw you just now, I thought I should come over."

Funny that he'd feel bad about the other day and not about how their relationship ended. "It's no big deal." She shrugged and half smiled, hoping she convinced him of her indifference. She could tell there was more he wanted to say, but she decided to gather her purse as if she intended to leave. She wanted him to know that he had no power or influence over her emotions.

"There was something else I wanted to say, if I may," he said.

"Go on."

"I may from time to time be coming down here to fill in for Father Goren, and I just don't want it to be awkward between us if I see you."

She smirked. "Father Goren is back this weekend, and the church is closing soon for the season. So I don't think I'll be seeing you for a long time at least."

"You didn't hear?"

She cocked her head.

"Father Goren will be gone for the final two weekends that the church is open. Yesterday, the hurricane hit the area where he's staying in Rhode Island. His sister's house was hit pretty badly."

"Isn't she in a hospice facility?"

"She is, but Father Goren sleeps at her house when he's down there. Because he's next of kin, he's expecting to deal with a few insurance claims on her behalf. I think it's his house to inherit."

How providential. Father Tristan just couldn't seem to stay away.

"I'll go to a different church. I was planning on it anyway, because, you know, this place isn't open year round." A part of her wanted to mention attending Jude's home church in Wells, but another part of her wanted to keep her personal life private and not invite any questions.

"I wish you wouldn't. This is your church. Father Joe is here, too. He'll be conducting the Saturday evening and Sunday noon Masses moving forward."

Violet nodded. "Good to know."

"I hope you don't feel like you have to go to Mass elsewhere."

"I just moved here. It's hardly my home parish," she explained, realizing that she started to give away more information about her life than she wanted. She hoped he wouldn't take it as an invitation to give her a summary of the past seven years of his life, either. She didn't want to know more about him or become mesmerized by his warm brown eyes again…because that hadn't ended well. She needed the conversation to end.

Another parishioner entered the church. Relieved, she hoped it was someone who would seek out Father Tristan and steal him away for a conversation or confession. Anything.

However, a middle-aged woman simply said hi and sat herself a few rows up from Violet. Now that they had company, Violet hoped Father Tristan would walk away.

She tried to avoid eye contact. It hurt too much to look into his eyes and see what their babies might have looked like. The doctor had confirmed she was having a girl and a boy. If they were alive now, they would be six years old. Who would they have looked more like? Would they each have a combination of Violet's blonde locks or Tristan's black hair? Her blue eyes or his? His dimples or her high cheekbones? But Tristan couldn't know any of her thoughts. She'd suffered with them, alone, long enough, and she wasn't about to open old wounds.

If she had just told Tristan sooner, would things have been different? Would they have been a family? She wanted to push all of the thoughts out of her head. She didn't need to fall down this rabbit hole for the one-thousandth time. She thought of Jude and relaxed a bit. She longed to be in his safe arms right now.

Father Tristan's eyes fell to her hand—her bare ring finger. She pulled her hand away and put it in her pocket, a bit embarrassed that after all of this time, she wasn't married. Not only had Tristan *not* wanted to spend his life with her, but no man since had made the move to do so, either, except possibly Jude. He seemed ready to tie the knot.

"Well, welcome to Maine." Father Tristan rose. Some of the tension slipped away as he stood to leave. "You'll be in my prayers," he said.

She half smiled, choosing not to say anything else. As he left the pew, he knelt and made the sign of the cross.

She exhaled as his footsteps softened the farther away he walked. But then they stopped. He cleared his throat and hurriedly walked back towards her. What now?

"Violet," he said. "I really need to talk to you about something."

Talk to me about what? "Ok? Let's go outside." Violet gestured to the woman trying to pray. She led the way out of the back doors into the September heat, with her heart racing. She stopped under the shade of a tree. "What's going on?"

Father Tristan sighed. "Seven years ago. I know it was a really rough time for you."

You literally have no idea.

"It felt like our relationship ended abruptly, and there was no closure."

She put her hands on her hips. "No, I'm pretty sure there was a definitive end."

"Violet, it was your sister. Sadie told me not to contact you. That's why you haven't heard from me all of this time."

"Well, it's nice to know that you can respect my sister's wishes but not mine." She made a mental note to scold Sadie later, but at the same time, she appreciated her protectiveness.

Father Tristan bit his lip. "You're right. I was an asshole."

"Yup." She folded her arms across her chest. "There's nothing left for us to discuss. You can go live with your clear conscience now. And by the way—" She pointed her finger straight at him. "You don't just get to admit you're an asshole and think that everything is ok now because it's not. As you always said, actions speak louder than words. Your actions were pathetic. It must've been so convenient for you that Sadie told you to stay away because then you didn't have to man up and apologize. Let me tell you, it's a heck of a lot easier for you to say sorry now that you wear that cloth."

Father Tristan stayed put as Violet turned her back and walked away. A part of her wanted him to come after her and beg for her forgiveness, but she wasn't going to turn around. He wasn't going to get the satisfaction. As soon as she was confident Tristan couldn't see her anymore, Violet called Sadie.

"So, when did you tell Tristan not to contact me?"

"Whoa, whoa. Back up! What happened? Did you run into him again?"

"Sadie, start talking." Her voice rose.

"Are you almost home?"

"Two minutes away."

"Let's just talk when you get back," Sadie pleaded.

"No! Right now. My entire world has been rocked! Thanks to you and *him*."

Sadie heaved a deep sigh. "Violet, I'm sorry. Truly, truly, truly. You know how I hate admitting I'm wrong. Clearly, I was wrong. I thought it would be best if you never heard from him again. I mean, you two were never going to end up together. Why give him the chance to try to win you back?"

"That wasn't your decision to make."

"I did it to protect you," she said. "He was no good for you, and you know that."

"He didn't even know I was pregnant! He had a right to know. Maybe if he had reached out, I would've told him, and all of this could be behind me." Violet yelled as she pushed open their front door. She hung up the phone as she walked toward the couch.

Sadie held out a glass of wine for Violet. She grabbed it and contemplated spilling it all over Sadie and/or their Auntie Rose's cream couch. How momentarily satisfying it would be. Sadie opened her mouth to respond.

"Don't say a word! I need to air my grievances first." Violet pointed her finger at Sadie and huffed. "That man-devil took something away from me that was never meant to be his. And all these years, I've been wondering why I never heard from him. No apology. He totally ghosted me." She broke into tears. She crumbled into Sadie's arms.

"Why? Why!?" Violet wailed. "I hate him. And look at him. He moves on with his life as if he's some pious priest. Everyone adores him! He doesn't live with what I live with. It's not fair! He deserves to feel this pain every day of his life!"

Sadie stroked Violet's hair, like their mother used to when they snuggled or had a bad day at school.

Violet started massaging her temples. "How could I ever tell him now?"

"You keep blaming yourself for losing the babies, and I've always told you, it's not your fault."

"That's not what the doctor said."

"That doctor was a prick," Sadie said. "He wasn't your ob-gyn. He was just some pompous ER doctor who clearly had a vendetta against women and wanted to make you feel bad."

Violet scrunched her face. Sadie was pretty funny when she described people she disliked. She wouldn't say it now, but she enjoyed it when Sadie broke up a serious moment with some humor.

"It doesn't change the fact that I made some very questionable choices that night, and I'd likely have carried my twins to term had I not done those things."

"You don't know that."

"It doesn't matter," Violet said. "I thought I was past all of this. Why does this keep blowing up in my face?"

"You keep carrying around this narrative that it's all your fault, and it's weighing you down," Sadie said. "You can change the narrative."

"You've been watching *Dr. Phil* again."

"No," Sadie laughed. "Actually, yes, I have been watching him, but that's beside the point. Stop deflecting."

"None of this weighed me down anymore, until Tristan waltzed back into my life."

"Ehh, I beg to differ. You've never really moved on."

Violet rolled her eyes.

"Vi, if you're going to act like this all was your fault for one foolish night of activities, then ok. Go ahead, blame yourself. But at least work on forgiving yourself so you can move on. Go to therapy. Do something. This self-pity can't last forever."

"Sadie, stop! It's so easy for you to say that because you're not the one who has to live with this every single day of your life."

"No, but I live with you, and you can be a pretty lousy sister sometimes."

"The feeling is mutual." Violet jumped up from the couch, blew her nose, and grabbed her keys. "I'm going for a walk on the Marginal Way. I want to be alone."

Was Sadie right? Her words about not having moved on pierced Violet's chest. It had been seven years. Time was supposed to heal, right? Had it?

* * * * *

Traffic was light on I-95 North as Father Tristan drove to Kennebunk. He stayed in the right lane driving the speed limit as the cars behind him merged to the left to pass. He was in no rush. What was there to go back to? The more he could prolong this drive, the better. Getting back to the rectory meant facing the temptation of Googling Violet. Then, he'd probably make a stupid decision, like finding a way to contact her (did he still have her number?) and see where the conversation would lead. She was a beautiful woman, and he felt like he could talk to her all day. That hadn't changed.

He punched the steering wheel, grazing the horn. He replayed their conversation in his head. What could he have said differently? Who was he kidding? It was the wrong place and the wrong time. Maybe it would never be the right time. Maybe he shouldn't have listened to Sadie and reached out to Violet years ago.

What would the parishioners think if they knew that, in his previous life, he treated his ex-girlfriend so terribly? To make matters worse, back then, he had been trying to wash away his problems with alcohol. It wasn't exactly role-model behavior for someone supposed to be *in persona Christi* as a priest. Then again, that was before he was a priest and there were saints, like St. Ignatius of Loyola and St. Augustine, who walked less-than-pious paths before converting.

Tristan took an early exit off 95 to drive back roads the rest of the way, extending his trip so he could think more. It was exactly what his father would do with him as a young boy. When he was old enough to realize they were taking "the long way home," he'd pester his dad as to why. Couldn't they just go home?

He was only twelve years old when he started to realize it was his dad's way of protecting him from seeing his mom in a drunken stupor. The twelve Mike's Hard Lemonade bottles he'd found hidden under his bed one afternoon after returning home from school didn't alarm him at first. He didn't know what "hard" meant. He just thought his mom was really thirsty and wanted some lemonade, which she told him he could have only on special occasions, like holidays and birthdays. When he brought the bottles downstairs, proud to help with recycling, his mom was horrified.

"Tristan! Where on God's green Earth did you get those?" Her mouth gaped open.

"I found them under my bed," he answered.

She broke down in tears, and his dad rushed over. "What's wrong? Tristan, let me have those," he said softly, taking each one and placing them in the recycling bin.

"I think your mom was in your room, putting away some clothes and cleaning up, and she must have gotten really hot and thirsty."

Tristan nodded his head, accepting the explanation. Why would his mom cry over this? What was so bad about it? Later on, he heard his mom and dad fighting. That was old hat, but this time, there was vitriol in his dad's voice that he'd never heard before.

"Bev, you can't go on like this. We can't live like this forever."

The next morning, his mom was gone. His dad hadn't run after her, but instead, he welcomed her with open arms the dozen or so times that she chose to return. He'd never understood his dad's allegiance to a woman who'd broken his heart multiple times over. His dad took their wedding vows seriously, but not his mom. Now, as a priest, Tristan knew he'd never have to face those same decisions.

If he had made amends with Violet years ago, maybe they'd be married now. It would have brought a whole host of complications, including trusting another person with his heart. The priesthood was simpler, right? No midnight feedings. No worries about providing financially for a family. No one to question his decisions. No addictions to forgive.

Chapter 7

Violet hadn't spoken to her spiritual director, Sister Maria, since she'd moved to Maine, but she promised to keep her updated about how life was going. So far, not so good. She called the convent where Sister Maria lived outside of Boston. The sweet nun who answered their general phone line said Sister Maria was not available. Violet left a short message and her cell phone number so that she could call her back.

Violet sauntered along the Marginal Way, planning to end in Perkins Cove for a lobster roll. The wind was unrelenting, but she didn't mind. It meant fewer people to contend with on the way. She stopped at various points to take a break on a bench or let her hair blow in the wind while she contemplated the rocks cascading into the ocean.

For the past seven years, Sister Maria was Violet's main link to the Catholic Church. Violet hadn't spoken to anyone from the young adult groups or the volunteer committees she'd been part of back when she and Tristan were dating. All of those relationships were a casualty of their break-up. Sister Maria encouraged Violet to see it differently: these people loved Violet for who she was, and they weren't going to shut her out because she no longer dated Tristan. Yes, it would be awkward to potentially see him at events, but he didn't have a monopoly on everyone they'd been friends with while they were together.

Violet understood Sister Maria's points, but she didn't want to risk running into him. It was just easier that way. She laughed to herself over the irony that she'd painstakingly tried to avoid him in Boston, only to move away and run into him in a confessional.

Her cell phone pinged. It was Sister Maria, thankfully.

"My Violet, how are you?"

"I've been better. How are you?" Violet walked over to one of the rocks overlooking the ocean and sat down.

"Still alive and grateful for it."

Violet smiled. At least someone was happy. "Sister Maria, I ran into Tristan." She ran her hand through her hair.

"Oh no! Dear, I'm so sorry. I should've told you he was a priest up there…"

"No, I'm glad you didn't because I probably would've second-guessed moving here. I don't want to live my life afraid of seeing him."

"Alright then. How is he, Father Tristan?"

Violet looked out at the people walking along the low tide. "Well, I barely spoke to him because he was my confessor, and then I bolted. I don't know, but it really rattled me."

"What a coincidence! Tell me how it upset you."

Violet loved Sister Maria's warm voice. "It just seemed that my life was going well literally up until that moment. I moved up here to be closer to Jude, as you know, and Sadie lives with me. I really like my new job. So, maybe life was just too good."

"How did seeing Father Tristan change that?"

"It just brought back these old memories, and I wonder if it's a sign from God."

"A sign of what?"

Violet smiled. Sister Maria had a way of making her feel understood without saying much. "I don't know. Like there's some unfinished business."

"Is there?"

"I've still never told him about the twins. I've confessed it and prayed about it, and I don't know what to do."

"That's why you're confused?"

"Mmhmm."

"My dear, I know you want me to tell you what to do, but God has given you free will."

Violet laughed. "In this instance, I wish he hadn't."

"How do you think you'll feel if you never tell Father Tristan about the twins?"

Her stomach dropped. "Probably pretty crummy."

"How do you think you'll feel if you do tell him?"

Violet sighed. "Definitely relieved, like a weight off my shoulders."

"Well, I think we have our answer then!"

Violet sighed. "I suppose. I just don't see what it would change. He's a priest. Could he be defrocked for that?"

Sister Maria laughed. "No, dear, not at all. He probably would not have been admitted into seminary if he had living children because the Church would expect him to take care of his own, but that's not the case in this situation."

Violet nodded, considering the possibility that had she not lost the twins, Tristan might not be Father Tristan.

Sister Maria continued, "Violet, how are *you*, my dear? Other than this situation? It sounds like you are loving life."

"Things are great, otherwise. I'm hoping Jude will propose soon. I think you'd like him."

"I'm sure I would. Remind me what he does for work again."

"He's a real estate agent on his family's team."

"Oh, yes! That's right." She pictured Sister Maria sitting in her blue, tufted chair at the convent, her eyes twinkling and her hands expressing all of her words.

"He's really good at it, but I think he'll eventually transition into a management role because he's tired of working weekends. For now, it works because I work weekends, too."

"And still during those crazy early morning hours?"

"Unfortunately, yes," Violet said. "But there's a lot of turnover here, so I'm hoping that within the next few months, I can move to daytime hours."

"With your work ethic and talent, I'm sure you will." Sister Maria's sincerity easily translated through the phone.

"Thanks." Violet felt a little guilty for not asking Sister Maria how she was doing yet. "So how's the women's home? Is it full?"

"It sure is! We're as busy as ever. We just had a newly pregnant teen move in. Her family threw her out when she told them about the baby."

"That's so sad," Violet said.

"It is too common, but I'm so grateful we can help women like her in their time of need."

"Sister Maria, sometimes when I hear what you do every day, and I think about what I do, it just doesn't compare. I feel like my job is silly comparatively."

"Violet, that's just the devil talking. All work has dignity because it's done by people who are made in the image and likeness of God. Mother Teresa said, 'It is not how much we do, but how much love we put in the doing.'"

Violet sighed. "You're so wise. Thanks for the reminder. I always feel better after I talk to you."

"Likewise, my dear Violet. How are Sadie and your mom?"

"They're both good. My mom is still working at the hospital full-time. Sadie is busy with school. Her compositions are amazing, but she's still not going to church. I don't know if she'll ever come back to the faith." Violet groaned.

Sister Maria laughed. "We can't control whether others believe. All you can do is pray for her and continue to live your life."

"Yea, I just feel like I've been a terrible example. I'm the Catholic girl who got pregnant before marriage and then lost the babies."

"Every saint has a past, and every sinner has a future," Sister Maria counseled.

Chapter 8

"You ready?" Violet's videographer, Paul, was a middle-aged, balding man who loved working mornings, for some reason. He was pretty quiet, but conversation flowed easily when asked about his wife and six kids.

"Yep, let me just run to the ladies' room."

She re-applied her lipstick and touched up her mascara. This morning, she would report from the station's SUV to show viewers the slippery road conditions. It was an easy assignment and didn't require any hard-hitting journalism, but it was popular with the audience. As she was always reminded, "Weather wins."

It was a distraction from everything else on her mind. Her conversation with Sadie left her feeling uneasy. What was she supposed to do? Should she tell Jude that she still found Father Tristan beguiling? She wasn't actually *doing* anything. She threw her bag into the back seat of the van and buckled up in the front.

"They're going to take us at the top of the five," Paul said.

"Sounds good. I can't wait for the day when top of the five means 5 p.m., not a.m."

Paul chuckled. "When that happens, you won't be reporting on the weather. You'll be doing something much more exciting."

They had about ten minutes to spare until her first live shot and shared small talk while Christmas music played in the background. Paul always let reporters pick which station to listen to in between their hits.

"Mic check," the director said into her ear.

"Good morning, Portland. It's a snowy morning here and—"

"Great."

Violet pulled down the passenger-side visor to double-check her appearance and make sure no hairs were out of place. What if Tristan were watching this morning? The thought made her stomach jolt, similar to the feeling she got approaching the peak of a rollercoaster, knowing a drop was imminent. She hated the feeling and wanted it gone.

"Coming to you in sixty," the morning show producer said into Violet's ear.

She laughed quietly, remembering her first years in television in Springfield, Massachusetts. She used to get so nervous before her live shots that she'd breathe into a paper bag. Now, she felt like she could have rolled out of bed five seconds before her hit and be fine.

She had a live shot scheduled for each block of the morning show. After doing her intro, Violet turned the camera away from herself and towards the road so that viewers could see the road conditions and simulate them driving along. She gave a description of the elements—snow, sleet, hail—as well as the name of the street. How many different ways could she say it was snowing? On mornings like this, most schools were closed or had a delayed opening, so the streets were fairly clear of cars.

After about ninety minutes, her producer called.

"Hey Rach, what's up?"

"We're going to re-route you and Paul. There's a fire in Kennebunk."

Finally, some real news. "Got it. Can you text the address?"

"Yea, I will. If you want to just search for it in Waze, it's the rectory in Kennebunk right by the beach."

* * * * *

Thirty-five minutes later, they pulled up outside the Saint Anthony Franciscan Friary. Flames engulfed one of the side buildings as plumes of smoke billowed into the crisp winter air. While crews hosed it down, Violet spotted the assistant fire chief. They hadn't officially met, but she'd seen him interviewed before on air. She went over to introduce herself.

"Hi, I'm Violet Marie."

"Nice to meet you. Assistant Chief Bergamot."

"We're setting up to do a live shot. What can you tell me about the fire?"

Violet's producer spoke into her earpiece that the live feed would come to them in about three minutes, as soon as they were back from the commercial break. Paul started to set up the shot, making sure that Violet was positioned properly in the frame so that people could see her and the dying fire at the same time.

"It started about forty minutes ago. One of the, uh, priests was apparently cooking some breakfast and forgot he left the stove on. Next thing he knew, the flames tore through the kitchen, and here we are."

"Is anyone hurt?"

"Not that I'm aware of. The priests are all huddled over there…praying."

"Ok, thanks. We're going live in less than a minute."

Violet did her segment walking toward the fire, which had reduced mostly to smoke. She informed the audience of the update from Assistant Chief Bergamot. There were no deaths or injuries and, in news, that meant it wasn't a big story. Violet hated that this was how the news worked, but she'd grown numb to it.

"Hey, Violet," Rachel said in her ear. "Any chance you can talk to one of the priests and do a live interview?"

"Yea, I'll try," Violet said.

"Great. Let's try that for your next hit."

Violet heaved a sigh. Walking toward the group of priests felt awkward. She knew Father Tristan was in the group. He'd gladly do a live TV interview, but she mentally crossed him off the list. Maybe she could talk to the priest who accidentally started the fire. No, that was too mean, but this was journalism, so technically, she'd at least pretend to seek out the instigator. She looked over at Paul and was instantly grateful for him. Father Tristan wouldn't bring up their last conversation in front of her co-worker, so she could just stay by Paul and not be left alone with Tristan. Father Tristan.

As she approached, bundled in her Channel 8 parka, Tristan emerged from the group of priests.

"Hey, are you ok?" Violet asked.

"Yea, we're all good."

She suddenly became self-conscious. Would Paul figure out that they knew each other? Who cared if he did? "Father Tristan, this is Paul. He's the best photog in Portland."

"Hardly," Paul said. "Nice to meet you, Father. I don't make it to Mass much, but praise God."

"Peace be with you."

"The assistant chief told me what happened. My producer wants me to do an on-camera interview with one of the priests."

"Are you asking me to do it?" Father Tristan smiled.

"No, I'm asking you if you can ask one of the other priests to do it."

"I can, but I doubt any of them will. I'm your best bet."

She rolled her eyes.

"Sixty seconds," Rachel said in her ear.

"Ok, fine. Stand right there. We're going to do a quick mic check."

"Violet, I need his name and his title and the spelling so we can put up a banner."

Violet passed the information on to Rachel. The interview was fairly short, with Father Tristan recounting how he was already awake when he heard the fire alarm and evacuated. He said none of the priests were hurt. It really wasn't as painful as Violet expected. He was strictly professional.

"Thanks, Violet," Rachel said afterward. "I think we're going to wrap it up there. The fire is out, and there's nothing left to report. By the way, that priest is hot."

Violet nodded. "I guess some people would think that." *Including me. Thank God Tristan can't hear any of this.* He started walking with Violet and Paul back to the news van.

"How's the priest who was cooking?" Violet asked.

"He's alright. Just embarrassed. Between you and me, I think he's losing his faculties. He's eighty-five. He should be retired, but with a shortage of priests, he's still filling in at least twice a month."

"Oh, poor guy."

"Violet…while I have you here, how would I go about getting an event covered by the news station?"

"It depends," Violet said. "What kind of event?"

"A charity event. We're collecting coats and scarves."

"Oh, are you talking about Warm-Up Wednesday?" Paul asked.

"Yes, exactly!"

"The station usually sends someone out to cover that," Paul said.

"Excellent. This is my first year here, so I'm new to it all," Father Tristan said. "I'm organizing it, and I guess the publicity falls to me, too."

"What's Warm-Up Wednesday?" Violet asked.

"It's a one-day event where the children at the local Catholic school collect hats and scarves to give to people in need, and then that night, there's a large charity dinner," Paul explained. "The Bishop usually attends, too, right?"

"Yes," Father Tristan answered.

Violet nodded and smiled weakly. "Sounds fun. Because the station already plans on covering it, I'm sure someone will reach out to you to coordinate."

"Can I give you my number, just in case?"

Violet didn't want to arouse suspicion with Paul, so she agreed and took out her work phone. Father Tristan rattled off his cell phone number. "I'll pass your number on to the assignment desk in case they want to get in touch with you," she said and quickly put her phone in her coat pocket.

* * * * *

"You and that priest fellow seemed familiar with each other," Paul stated as he drove I-95 back to the station. "You rattled off his name and how to spell it without even asking him."

She knew he was fishing for information, and she would make him work for it. "Yea, I've met him before."

"*Just* met him?"

More like made babies with him, but they didn't need to go there. "Yea, we've crossed paths a handful of times."

"So, he's an old boyfriend?" Paul inquired.

She laughed and glanced over at him. "Oh jeez, Paul. Was it that obvious?"

"I have an eye for these things. He seemed to care about you."

"He's a priest, so he should care about everyone," she said. How could she steer the conversation away from this?

"I'm sure he does, but I think he cares *extra* for you," Paul said.

"Be that as it may, Paul, I'm hopefully getting engaged soon. And he's a priest."

"Yea, well priests have eyes and feelings, too."

"I'm sure they do."

The snow lightened up with the morning rush in full force now, as people traveled into Portland for work. As much as she hated waking up early, Violet was glad that her hours were all off-peak as far as traffic was concerned.

"Are we back on snowcam duties?" Paul asked.

Thank God we've moved on from talk of Tristan. "No, they told me to just head back to the studio."

"Excellent. By the way, you're probably going to end up covering that Warm-Up event."

"Really?"

"Well, you work Wednesdays, right?"

"Yes."

"Yea, so the girl who used to have your job covered it every year. It's the biggest coat drive in the Portland area. So, I guess you'll see your ex again."

She nervously laughed and started inspecting the dirt underneath her fingernails. "Oh boy."

"It's good to be friends with a priest," Paul said. "I hear it's like a fast pass to Heaven."

"You don't have to worry about that. You have six kids. That's your fast pass."

"It doesn't feel very fast," Paul replied. Violet thought of his kids and whether she'd get the chance to have a family like his. As she pictured life with Jude, they fell into silence. She said a silent thank you to God that they had changed the subject. She didn't want to give clues to her interest in seeing Father Tristan again. She wanted to appear unaffected. *Oh, I saw my ex? So what. He likes me? So what. He hates me? So what. His opinion doesn't matter to me.*

Paul wasn't one to gossip. He was too preoccupied with being a dad to snicker about workplace drama or who's dating who. There was close to a one hundred percent chance he wouldn't mention her ex to anyone in the newsroom. But still. She felt it wise to hide her affection. Was that what she called it? Maybe it was just attraction? Objectively, any woman would find Father Tristan handsome. Surely, it was natural to enjoy the company of a man so striking. But was it more than that? How could she just forget their relationship and everything he'd done and said?

"Don't go, don't go, don't go, don't go," she remembered him pleading to her one night, his breath reeking of beer. They were on the couch, tangled in each other's arms, and Violet had just said it was time for her to go home.

"What do you mean? Don't go now or ever?" she'd asked.

"Both," Tristan replied. "Every woman I've ever loved has left me."

Violet saw a flash of vulnerability that night. Then, he didn't respond to her texts for five days. So much for him not wanting her to go. It left her confused and unsure for days. What happened to the wounded man on the couch who just wanted her company? Why had he gone cold? Did he even remember saying that to her? Probably not because he was drunk.

When Violet and Paul returned to the station, the assistant news director asked to see Violet in his office. "Are you comfortable emceeing events?" Bill liked to cut right to the chase.

"Yes," Violet said. She'd learned well to never turn down an opportunity.

"Excellent! I'm going to have you emcee an event in a couple of weeks. The girl you replaced used to do it every year. It's a daytime and evening event, so you'll work the third shift that day. It's called Warm-Up Wednesday. Are you familiar with it?"

"Paul was just telling me about it." *And so did Tristan.*

"Great. I'll let him get you up to speed on how it works. You'll have a great time, and I'll make sure Paul works the event, too. I'll put you in contact with the organizer. It's some new priest this year. Father something or other. He'll be your day-of contact." *Of course he would be; my life is a joke.*

Their run-ins were becoming too frequent to seem coincidental. Was this going to be par for the course from now on? Moving here was supposed to put Violet farther away from her past, not closer.

Chapter 9

"Running a couple of minutes late. Couldn't find my phone," Violet texted.

"Shocking!" Jude wrote back with a winky face.

Violet found Jude inside Joshua's, a local farm-to-table restaurant, about ten minutes later. Her body finally relaxed. She had tomorrow off because of an extra shift she'd worked the previous week, so no early wake up, and maybe they could take a walk together after dinner.

In general, Tuesdays weren't a busy night for the restaurant, but it was especially quiet now around 5 p.m. Most diners didn't arrive for at least another hour, but Jude insisted on an early dinner tonight.

His eyes lit up like a newly decorated Christmas tree as Violet approached. He stood to kiss and hug her when she reached the table. Her heart gave an extra pitter-patter at his joyous reaction.

He pushed the bread basket toward her. "I saved you the honey wheat rolls."

"Yes!" Violet cheered. She tore one of the warm brown rolls in half and smeared it with butter. "I'm so hungry! Should I stick with the usual or try something new?" She scanned the black leather-bound menu.

"Whatever makes you happy."

"I both love and hate when you say that because it's not helping me decide what to get. What are you going to order?"

"Filet."

"Good! I'll have a couple bites."

"As you always do."

"Oh c'mon," Violet patted his hand. "On our first date, I didn't help myself to any of the food on your plate."

"True, but you eyed it like a hawk." He sipped his wine.

The waiter came over and took their orders. Fifteen minutes later, he brought out their food. Violet squealed as she looked at the haddock with its caramelized onion crust. Growing up, she wasn't used to more than a monthly meal at the local diner, but Jude had a much more discerning palate and had broadened her culinary world.

Before taking a bite of the haddock, she reached across the table with her fork and speared a mini potato from Jude's plate.

"So good!" she gushed. "I'm savoring the moment, but honestly I can't wait for dessert. I'm going to order the walnut tart with maple ice cream."

"Let me guess, you want me to get the fudge cake so you can have a couple bites?"

"You know me so well." Their banter brought an uplifting levity to the night. Violet took a moment to notice his chiseled jaw and high cheekbones. Sometimes, she couldn't believe he'd chosen her and accepted her flaws. When the waiter came by a few minutes later, she asked him to doggy bag the rest of her dinner.

"Want to take a walk after?" Jude asked.

"Yes," Violet gushed as the waiter placed her tart a la mode and Jude's cake in front of them.

Could life always be this simple and fun: a casual dinner at a slightly upscale, but still homey restaurant followed by a walk. After Jude paid the check, they walked hand in hand, their fingers intertwined, down Post Road. It reminded her of the first time Jude reached for her hand just over a year ago on this very road. It was gentle and slow, but she felt an electricity shoot up her arm. She hadn't made a big deal of it but instead squeezed his hand back. Now, hand-holding for them was old hat, and she wondered if she'd taken it for granted.

Whenever she was single and saw other couples holding hands, she swelled inside hoping that it would be her someday: a man would effortlessly wrap his fingers around hers and proclaim to the world that they were committed to each other. A certain finger, after all, was where one displayed a life-long commitment of marriage to the whole world.

"We should try that coffee shop sometime." Violet pointed across the street. "It looks cute."

"Sounds great." Jude seemed quiet, with a faraway, pensive look, since they left the restaurant.

"Are you ok? You seem a little off."

"Yea, I'm good." He took a deep breath. "Actually, can we sit for a minute? It's just been a long day, and that food, as good as it was, is putting me into a coma."

"Of course." Violet's pulse quickened.

They sat down on the nearest bench, and she rested her head on his shoulder and shut her eyes. He wrapped his right arm around her shoulder as she nestled in, catching a whiff of his aftershave.

"Shoot, Vi, I think I left my phone at the restaurant." He patted his coat pockets with his right hand.

"Let's go back and get it before they close." Violet stood and turned.

"Violet," Jude said as she strode ahead of him. His voice was warm.

She turned around.

He was down on one knee. "I love you so much. Will you marry me?"

She'd wanted this moment for so long. She stared into his chocolate eyes, the streetlights reflecting off his irises. Her hand clutched her chest.

"Yes!"

Jude placed a pear-shaped diamond ring onto her left ring finger. She gasped at the diamond's brilliance. How did he know what she'd wanted? Sadie? Speaking of which, Sadie should be her first call. Had he asked her mom for her hand in marriage?

Jude scooped Violet up and spun her around. She threw her head back, laughing.

"You want to marry me? You really want to marry me?" she asked.

"Every day."

A surge of relief washed over her. Jude knew her darkest secret and still wanted to spend the rest of his life with her.

"Wait, did you really leave your phone at the restaurant?"

"No. I just couldn't think of a creative way to get you walking ahead of me."

Violet cradled his stubbled chin in her hand. "You're such a dork, but I love you."

* * * * *

"Miss Violet," the little girl said. It was Friday afternoon, Violet's version of a Sunday night since her workweek started on Saturdays. "Miss Violet!" She pulled on her skirt.

"Yes, Harper." Violet crouched down.

Harper rubbed her eyes. "I missed you so much! Can I have a hug?"

"Of course." Violet's heart swelled. She didn't share with her boss that she volunteered at the youth center because she knew she'd soon be followed by a TV crew to broadcast her efforts. The idea of publicizing it repulsed her. She always rolled her eyes at celebrities who made sure their community service was well documented. She didn't understand the impulse to shout, "Look at me! I volunteer!" But it was all about optics in TV, and she knew her news director would take any chance to paint one of his reporters in a positive light. That's exactly what next week would bring with Warm-Up Wednesday.

Violet pulled Harper close and hugged her.

"I like your dress," Harper said.

"Thank you!"

"Do you want to see my dolls?"

"Absolutely!"

"Ok, come over here," Harper said. "Follow me."

Violet loved Harper's take-charge attitude. She had no inhibitions. Harper led the way into the youth center's playroom. She showed off a set of American Heritage dolls. "This one is named Lily," Harper explained, holding up a blonde doll with blue eyes. "I think she looks like you."

Violet's stomach dropped. She hoped Harper wouldn't detect her uneasiness, but kids were so perceptive. "What a beautiful name you picked for her! Where did you come up with that?"

"I hear my mom say her favorite flower is a lily. My mom loves lily flowers. Do you wanna hold her?" Harper asked. "Here you go."

Violet accepted the Lily doll and started brushing her blonde hair with the tiny comb. *Lily, my lily. That was supposed to be her name; that is her name. I never got to comb her hair. I never got to hold her or John Paul. It's all my fault.*

"Miss Violet, I like your ring. It's so pretty."

Violet snapped herself out of her trance and eyed the pear-cut diamond on her left hand. "Thank you."

"Is it from your mom?"

Violet shook her head. "No. Actually it's from my fiancé."

"What's a fancy?"

Violet laughed. "A fiancé is the person you're going to marry."

"You're going to get married!?"

"Yea, isn't that so cool?" Violet asked.

"Wow!" Harper squealed. "When is your wedding? Tomorrow?"

"I wish. We haven't picked a date yet, but it will be soon." Violet loved Harper's exuberance, which always energized her after leaving the rec center.

"Do I get to come?" Harper asked.

"Do you want to come?" She hadn't told anyone other than Jude, but Harper had been in the back of her mind as an ideal flower girl.

"I've never been to a wedding before," Harper said.

"We'll have to talk to your mom about it."

"She'll say yes."

Violet marveled at Harper. "That's great. Ok, I know you want to play with Lily and her doll friends, but why don't we read a book and then come back and play later?"

"Ok," she shrugged and flipped her light brown hair over her shoulder.

One of Violet's tasks was to help Harper with her reading. She'd taken a special interest in Harper over the last month because, like Violet, she was dyslexic. Harper was too young to really understand. More so than a teacher, Violet understood what Harper was going through. Even if they didn't talk about dyslexia specifically now, Violet wanted Harper to know that as she grew up, she could answer questions. Dyslexia was part of why Violet worked in TV. As much as she loved journalism, she had struggled with the typing and printing aspect of it. To consume news, she much preferred radio and TV. So it seemed like a natural fit when it came time to select a major in college.

About an hour later, Harper ran over to mom, who had just arrived. "Mommy! Guess what?"

"What, sweetie?" Hannah, Harper's mom, asked. She scooped Harper into her arms.

"Miss Violet is having a wedding!"

"I got engaged earlier this week." Violet blushed.

"Congratulations!"

"Mommy, Miss Violet said I can go to her wedding."

"Did she, now?" Hannah winked at Violet. "We'll have to see if you're free on her big day."

"We haven't picked a date yet," Violet said. "But hopefully we'll know within the next couple of weeks after we look at venues."

"Mom, I'm so excited for Miss Violet! Look at the ring she got from her fancy."

"Honey, I think the word you're trying to say is fiancé," Hannah enunciated. Violet held out her hand. "That is stunning, Violet. Did he pick that himself?"

"I think he may have had a little help from his five sisters. He's one of seven kids."

"Wow, God bless his mother," Hannah said. "We're so happy for you."

Hannah put Harper down, and she ran off toward her dolls. "Violet, you don't need to invite Harper to your wedding. You know how she just asks any question that pops into her head."

"I love that about her. I was already planning on inviting you all." Harper talked about her dad a lot, but Violet had never met him. She had the feeling that Harper was a daddy's girl.

"We really appreciate that."

Harper walked back with all of her dolls. "Thank you for gathering all of those up, sweetie."

"Do we get to go to Friendly's?" Harper asked.

"Yea, Daddy's already on his way, and we'll meet him there."

"Yay! Mom, can Miss Violet come with us?"

"If she wants to," Hannah replied.

"Harper, that is so kind of you to invite me, but I actually have to go home and go to bed now."

"Bed? But it's not even dark outside!"

"I know, but I have to wake up very, very early in the morning for work."

"How early?" Harper asked.

"Around one-thirty."

Harper's eyes bulged. "One-thirty in the morning? I've never been awake that early!"

"I wish I could say the same." Violet smiled at Hannah.

"Alright, Harper, let's say goodbye to Miss Violet so she can go home."

"Bye." Harper hugged Violet around her legs. "I'm going to get a big sundae at dinner."

"That sounds so good!" Violet said. "See you next week."

"Thanks so much for everything," Hannah said.

"My pleasure."

Violet watched them walk out. Her long-awaited dream of having a family with Jude and going out to dinner with their own little crew was getting much, much closer to becoming a reality. Still, her stomach clenched with a gnawing feeling that babies might not be in her future. What if God was so mad at her for what happened that he made her infertile? Or she had multiple miscarriages? She knew God didn't work that way; infertility wasn't a punishment. Yes, it was a tremendous cross to bear, but it wasn't retribution for sins. Still, her chest ached at the thought of not ever being pregnant again or being the reason Jude might never hold his own child.

Chapter 10

Violet and Sadie carpooled to Newburyport, Massachusetts to go dress shopping with their mom after Violet's shift on Saturday. The town's bridal shop was a midway point for them. Gloria Rosati could not stop saying how thrilled she was to shop in Newburyport, which she invariably described as the perfect location for a nautical New England Hallmark Channel movie.

"How about this one?" Gloria squealed, grasping an ivory, long-sleeved wedding gown with a turtleneck.

"Long sleeves? She's getting married in July. Do you want her to melt?" Sadie asked. "Vi, look at this one!" Sadie pulled out a white tube top dress that looked like it hung only to the mid to upper thigh.

"You two!" Violet chastised. "Mom wants me in a parka, and Sadie wants me to dress like a hooker."

"Girls, please." Their mom held up her hand in her famous "traffic cop" fashion, as Violet and Sadie called it.

Violet took another lap around the store, stopping at different dresses that caught her eye. Her heart stopped when she reached the flower girl dresses. They were so tiny and sweet. She and Jude didn't have any nieces or nephews yet, so hopefully Harper was up to the task.

Violet closed her eyes and hugged one of the dresses. If her twins had lived, Lily could be wearing this dress right now. She imagined dressing her in a frilly, little white dress and tying her hair up with a bow. Then again, would she even be dress shopping right now if she hadn't lost the twins? Would she have married Tristan instead? Would she have ever met Jude?

Sadie called Violet over to look at another gown. She tried on more than a dozen dresses, but she couldn't see herself walking down the aisle in any of them. When she plopped onto the pink loveseat at the bridal boutique, the frantic shop assistant rushed over with some other options.

"I appreciate it, but I think I'm all set for now," Violet told her.

"Are you ok?" her mom inquired.

Violet's face felt warm. "I'm just feeling a little overwhelmed."

"C'mon, Vi! This is supposed to be fun, not stressful," Sadie chided.

"So, why do I feel so stressed?"

"Because you are always in your head. I don't know what goes on in between those two ears of yours, but I'd remove your overthinking defect if I could."

"Nothing felt right about those dresses."

"Honey, we're at the first shop," Gloria reassured her, stroking her hair. "You don't have to find your wedding dress here."

"I know," Violet said, "but it doesn't even feel exciting to me. I dread the thought of going somewhere else and doing this all over again."

"And let me guess, because you're not feeling 'excited enough,' you're panicking that this must mean something!" Sadie used her fingers as quotation marks for emphasis.

Violet rolled her eyes.

"Sadie…" their mom started.

"She's right," Violet said. "Something feels off."

"Are you about to get your period?" she whispered. Violet was fifteen years past the stage of a menstrual cycle being awkward, but her mom still spoke of it discreetly. Violet shook her head and spotted the tiny flower girl dresses with matching shoes again.

"Are you pregnant?" Her mom lowered her voice even more.

"No," Violet snapped. "I just thought I'd be more excited about all of this."

"Vi, what do I keep telling you about expectations?" Sadie asked. "You have these sky-high ideas of what should happen, and then when life inevitably disappoints you, you feel crushed."

"Let's just call it a day."

"As you wish, Bridezilla," Sadie bowed to Violet.

Violet couldn't put her finger on her lack of motivation. Was it because she didn't feel like she deserved Jude's love? Or was it because she still hadn't told Tristan about the twins? How could she feel so unsettled when what she'd always wanted was finally within her grasp?

Chapter 11

Violet looked smashing, if she could say so herself.

Her midnight blue, solo strap floor-length dress was accented by a crystal barrette that held her updo in place and her engagement ring, that sparkling gem on prominent display on her ring finger. She believed it was an unmistakable sign to the world that yes, there was a man out there who loved her and found her worthy to spend the rest of his life with.

At the same time, she felt kind of silly. They were raising money for children whose families couldn't afford coats, and here she was wearing a designer dress and heels, promoting a look of luxury. Granted, she'd bought the dress and shoes secondhand, but still. Why her boss made her dress to the nines was beyond her.

It wouldn't look as glamorous, she supposed. Was that the point of these charity galas, anyhow? She couldn't fixate on existential thoughts now. She needed to focus on her job. "Just show up and look pretty," her news director, Bill, had advised.

The afternoon of coat collecting had gone well. Thankfully, no heels were required for that event—just winter boots, jeans, and a WMTW Channel 8 parka. They'd collected over six hundred coats and raised about seven thousand dollars so far. Violet had interviewed various people involved in organizing the event, including Father Tristan. Outside of that, they managed to exchange only a few cordial words the whole afternoon. Violet couldn't put a finger on their interactions. It wasn't icy, but was it professional? Tense? Maybe she was overthinking it.

Paul had been there all day, collecting b-roll of people dropping off coats in the city's public library parking lot. Father Tristan thanked each person, and every time she looked over, he seemed engrossed in conversation. She remembered from their days in love how when he talked to her, he made her feel like the only person in the world. Too bad the times they did see each other were few and far between, as he flaked on plans often. But when it was good, it was good.

She'd worn gloves the whole day, so there's no way he saw her engagement ring, but tonight he would. Her two-hour break in between the coat collection and the evening events gave her time to strategize all the ways she could keep her conversations with Father Tristan to a minimum. So far, he'd brought mostly strife to her life, and she didn't want any of that tonight. She had to say some opening words, thank all of the organizers, introduce the night's speakers, announce the silent auction winners, and smile. And look pretty.

She exchanged pleasantries with more than a dozen people who she knew she wouldn't remember later, but at least it kept an invisible fence between her and Father Tristan. Every minute she talked to someone else was one less minute she worried about talking to him.

"Hey, that looks new," Father Tristan pointed to her ring.

Violet jumped at his sudden appearance next to her. "Is that your way of saying congratulations?"

"I'm sorry," he said. "Yes, you're right. Congratulations. I'm happy for you."

"Thanks."

"Who's the lucky guy?"

"His name is Jude." He didn't need to know the last name.

"Might I have seen him at church?"

Subtle. She shrugged. "I doubt it. He goes to Saint Mary's in Wells."

"Well, I'm glad he's Catholic. I know that was always important to you."

"Yup." She took a sip of her water, hoping that either of them would find a way to end this conversation by the time she swallowed her drink. "Look, I'm sorry for my outburst the other day," she said. "It's obvious that we're going to run into each other from time to time, and I want it to be friendly. Our past is in the past."

"I agree. No need to worry about the other day."

She nodded. "The coat drive was awesome."

"Thank you. Everyone enjoyed your emceeing."

She shrugged and tried to hide her blush. "Just doing my job." When he didn't offer a reply, she continued. "I'm going to head out. I'm sure I'll see you around." She tucked a piece of hair behind her ear with her left hand. Had she done it on purpose to give him one last look at her ring? She wasn't sure.

Chapter 12

"Thanks for bringing me along." Sadie, Violet, and Jude all rode in his car to check out wedding venues. "I know how much you two value my opinion."

Violet rolled her eyes. "Yes, of course, Sadie."

"So am I getting a finder's fee?" Sadie grinned.

"A finder's fee for what?"

"For setting the two of you up on a blind date. I'm the reason you're getting married." It was true: Sadie and Jude had a mutual friend, Leonard, who Sadie met through the music scene in Boston. When Sadie went to Leonard's wedding about two years ago, she met Jude and instantly thought of Violet.

"She raises a good point, Vi," Jude said.

"Thank you, Jude," Sadie said. "I always knew you were a reasonable man. Violet?"

"Considering that you remind me constantly, and considering that I've never offered you anything more than, 'Thank you,' you can safely assume that there will be no finder's fee."

"At least I asked," Sadie said. "Can't fault me for that."

"Nope, and I'm sure it won't be the last time. Love you, sis."

Sadie huffed. "What's the name of the place we're going to again?"

"The Red Barn."

"I wouldn't peg you two as the farming type."

Jude laughed. "You've never seen me with a plow, have you?" He cocked his neck to see Sadie through the rearview mirror. She giggled. Sadie and Jude's friendly banter put her at ease. Sadie had never liked Tristan, so it was a relief when she and Jude hit it off immediately.

"Oh my gosh, this place is ex-pen-sive!" Sadie whistled as she scrolled through her phone. "Did you see the per-head price?"

Jude and Violet exchanged a look. Sadie knew Jude was wealthy, or rather his parents were wealthy, but she didn't know *how* wealthy. Truthfully, Jude told Violet he didn't really know numbers, either. He knew his family's wealth was in a certain range, but it wasn't typically discussed within the family. The understanding was simply that his family would pay for their children's college educations and weddings.

"It certainly is pricey, but you only get married once." Violet smiled at Jude and squeezed his hand on the center console. He'd told her not to worry about the cost. They could have a small wedding if that's what she wanted, but Jude also wanted her to know that she could dream bigger.

"Must be nice to marry rich," Sadie sighed.

"Sadie!" Violet chastised. But she knew Jude wasn't offended in the least.

"Are you dating anyone?" Jude asked.

Sadie rolled her eyes. "Not really. You know, dates here and there. Not many winners at Southern Maine."

"Have you tried Catholic Match?"

"Jude, when have I ever given you the impression that I wanted to date a Catholic?"

Violet laughed. "Yea, I think you have to have attended church at least once in the last decade to use the site."

"First of all, I go on Christmas and Easter when Mom makes me. Secondly, I don't think a guy who is super into his faith would consider someone like me, who could care less."

"True, but maybe you'd end up—"

"Don't even say it. I'm not going to church," Sadie said. "Your wedding is an exception, of course."

Violet held up her hands. "Alright, alright, I'll back off."

For the rest of the ride, they reviewed the preliminary guest list as Sadie added color commentary about everyone who was invited. When they pulled into the Red Barn, Gloria was already there, standing next to her car, in her favorite faux leather black jacket, scrolling through her phone.

* * * * *

After the tour, they debriefed at a local pub. No matter what, Violet and Jude promised that they wouldn't put a deposit down anywhere without sleeping on it at least one night. It didn't make the wedding salesperson too happy.

"Lunch is on me, ladies," Jude smiled. "This is great that we're all together. It doesn't happen often enough." He put his arm around Violet.

"So here's my one concern with the Red Barn..." Gloria started.

Violet and Sadie exchanged an eye roll and smirked. It was never just *one* concern with their mom. "I saw that, girls," she said. "Here's the thing, it's a gorgeous location, but if you're going to focus so much of your reception outside, you run the risk with the weather. I'd just hate to see you plan so much of your evening outside and then have it ruined by rain."

"That's actually a good point, Mom," Sadie said.

"I don't know. What do you think?" Violet turned toward Jude.

"I hadn't thought about it until just now, but I guess we have to decide if we're willing to risk it. I'll leave it up to you."

"It's your wedding, too."

"I've got all that matters right here." Jude raised Violet's hand.

Sadie reached for a garlic knot in the basket and rolled her eyes. "Ok, we get it. You're in looooove. Where is the waiter? I need a Corona."

They each thumbed through the plastic menus. "I don't know why I even look. I already know I'm getting fish and chips," Violet said.

"Same," Sadie said. "Mom, what diet are you on this week?"

She shook her head. "Keto."

"And that means you can eat...what exactly?"

"Basically, high-fat foods, almost no carbs."

Sadie pretended to gag. "Don't mind me if I help myself to another roll then." Sadie reached for the bread basket.

"I'll probably get a burger on a bed of lettuce with some mayonnaise."

"That sounds splendidly scrumptious," Sadie joked.

Gloria sat back in her chair and folded her hands on the table. "Isn't it amazing to think that this time next year you might be pregnant, Vi?" she asked. "No pressure, but I can't wait to be a grandma." Violet knew her mom didn't mean to trigger thoughts of the twins, but it didn't take much. Her heart felt heavy for a moment.

"You never let me forget." Violet turned to Jude, and he gave her an encouraging smile. He knew she was thinking of Lily and John Paul.

"Alright, we don't need to talk about procreation. What's the next place we're going to check out?" Sadie asked.

Violet mouthed a silent "thank you" to Sadie for changing the subject.

Jude stroked his chin a couple of times. "It's a banquet hall in Portland. I forget the name of it."

"Ocean Gateway." Violet forced a smile, wondering if this parade of venues could end sooner. She was relieved when the waiter came to take their orders. Sadie opted for a vodka tonic after the waiter informed her that they did not have Corona. As soon as he left, the wedding talk continued. "So, are you going to get married at St. Mary's in Wells?" Gloria asked.

"That's the plan," Violet answered. "Ideally, the venue will be close to the church."

"Ocean Gateway is about forty minutes from Wells, so it's a little farther than we'd like," Jude said.

"Well, how about Kennebunkport? There are so many options there, I'm sure." Gloria sipped her water while Violet considered the idea.

Violet groaned. "I know. There are so many decisions to make. Can we talk about something else for now?"

"Looks like Bridezilla is making another appearance. I knew she'd be here sooner or later," Sadie cackled.

Gloria shook her head. "My girls are both in their thirties, and they still act like little girls sometimes. You'll see someday when you have kids."

Violet frowned. *If we can have kids. Maybe we'll suffer as a childless couple as punishment for all that I've done.*

* * * * *

"Everything ok, Vi?" Jude asked. They sat on the rocking chairs outside her house after returning from lunch. It was their first time alone all day. "I could tell you were distracted today. Is it about the twins?"

She folded her arms across her chest and nodded.

"Are you still beating yourself up?"

"No," she said. "I mean, yes, of course, but that's not what's bothering me today."

"What is it, then?" Jude stroked Violet's hand, his eyes exuding his usual patience.

"I still haven't told Tristan. I think it would be a weight off my shoulders. I've been carrying this around for so long."

"I get it."

"But how do you feel about me telling him?" she asked.

Jude let out a deep breath. "I don't love the idea of you two being alone together, but I understand why you want to tell him. I want you to get this off your chest because I can see how much it's weighing you down. So if talking to him one-on-one is what you need to do, then do it."

"You mean that?"

"It's not fun for me to think about you two together, but the bigger payoff is that you'll be at peace. That's more important to me than my own discomfort."

"Thanks. Having your support means everything, though a part of me wishes you'd tell me not to talk to him and then it would be case closed."

Jude lifted her chin. "I know you, Vi, and you'd tell him anyway."

Chapter 13

Violet paced around the bungalow, biting her nails, a habit she'd only recently borrowed from Sadie. *Ugh.* Was she really going to go through with this? Did it even matter? Then she remembered what Jude said. "They were his babies, too. He deserves to know."

"Are you sure you want to do this?" Sadie asked.

"Don't talk me out of it. I need a pep talk now, not more confusion."

"Honestly, I don't understand your intent. Yes, they were his babies, too, but what changes if he finds out now?"

"It's not for me to decide. He's an adult," Violet said. "He can do what he wants with the information, but I have to tell him."

"Why don't I drive you over? You need to get this shit-show over with. I can wait in the parking lot close by and be your getaway driver, if need be."

Violet laughed. "That's not a bad idea. I feel like if you drive me, I won't talk myself out of this, and I don't want to."

Wrapped in her parka and snow boots, Violet found Sadie's car doors iced shut, one of the main downsides of not having a garage in the New England winter. She ran back inside to heat a mug of water and then doused it on the car. The ice cracked, popped, and broke free. Violet pulled her coat sleeve over her hand to act as a makeshift glove and pulled an ice scraper from Sadie's car. The tension eased out of her body with each ice pellet she speared and pushed off the car's windshield.

Sadie came out a couple minutes later. "Thanks for getting the car going. I'll get the back windows."

Violet almost didn't want Sadie's help. The longer it took, the longer she could put off telling Tristan the truth. Could the car possibly get stuck in the snow, and then Violet would be forced to reschedule? Could God help a girl out here?

But she knew. She'd been waiting for this to finally reveal her secrets, remove the pressure from her chest, and stop feeling the burden of it all. After this, she could marry Jude in peace. She'd never have to speak to Father Tristan again. No more what-ifs or what-could-have-beens.

A couple minutes later, Violet settled into the passenger seat and took a deep breath. Her heart racing from handling the snow but her face still cold, she welcomed the enveloping warmth of the heat blowing inside the car. In less than five minutes, Sadie pulled into the parking lot outside of the Backyard Coffee House. She squeezed Violet's hand as she idled the car along the sidewalk.

"Knock 'em dead."

"I don't think that expression really applies here."

"I know, but I thought it might lighten the mood, and based on your sullen expression, you could use it."

"Well, I appreciate your attempts at humor."

Violet unbuckled herself and stepped out of the car onto the slushy sidewalk. She peered into the coffee shop, wondering if Tristan was inside. Had he already spotted her? Adopting a calm and casual demeanor, she stomped her boots against the coarse, black entrance mat at the front door. Father Tristan waved from the corner. *Here we go.*

"Hey Violet, good to see you again. Was that your sister?" He stood as she took off her coat and hat and placed them over the chair between them.

"Yep. She had to run some errands in the area," Violet lied.

"I got you your favorite." Father Tristan pushed a steaming mug of black coffee toward her. It was nice that he remembered her beverage of choice, but she wouldn't let him charm her once again.

"Thank you." Violet folded her frigid fingers around the mug, sending a wave of heat through her body.

"How is Sadie?"

"She's doing well. She's enjoying Southern Maine, and the music she's composing is really, really good."

"That's great. She's very talented."

How much longer would this small talk continue? She took a long, slow sip of the black coffee, wishing Tristan had poured some whiskey in it, though she doubted priests were allowed to carry flasks.

"So, there's something I want to talk to you about." She caught his gaze for a flicker and sniffled to keep her Rudolph nose from running. "This is really hard for me to talk about, and quite honestly, I contemplated not even telling you."

Tristan nodded slowly.

Her eyes stung, and she sniffled again. "Um…" She bit her lip and fixed her stare on a nearby painting of a swan. She briefly wished she was a swan, with no romantic feelings or tough conversations to face.

"Violet, it's ok. You don't have to."

She turned her focus to the coffee in the mug, catching a bit of her own reflection in the black liquid. *Here goes nothing.*

"Tristan, about two weeks after we broke up, I found out I was pregnant."

Tristan swallowed, his Adam's apple bobbing up and down. She took his silence as permission to continue.

"With the way our relationship ended, I didn't want to tell you. I didn't think you'd care. I thought you might try to talk me into an abortion, which I knew I would never do. I was scared and ashamed, but I was determined to have the baby and either put him or her up for adoption or raise the baby myself. About twelve weeks in, another big surprise came. I was having twins. My heart sank and filled with joy at the same time. Suddenly, it felt insurmountable to raise them on my own, but that's what I wanted. Sadie was the most supportive person in all of this and vowed to help me. Sister Maria also offered to let me live at her home for pregnant mothers. Anyway, none of it mattered because six weeks later, I miscarried. I won't describe that level of despair, but because they were your babies, too, I just thought you should know."

Violet's forehead throbbed as she tried to stifle her sobs and keep people from looking over. Why had she ever thought it was a good idea to have this talk in public? "And I'm sorry it took me seven years to tell you," Violet said.

He reached for Violet's hand, but she recoiled and folded her arms across her chest. She'd said her peace. Could Sadie come back now?

Tristan cleared his throat and shifted in his seat. He reached for his back pocket and took out a tattered black wallet. He thumbed through it, eventually pulling out a yellow piece of paper. "Violet, I know. I've known all this time."

"What?"

He slid the note across the table. "You need to see this."

She covered her hand over her mouth. "How?" she asked.

"I got it in the mail with no return address."

"When? There's no date." *Who would've done this?*

"It was about three months after we broke up."

Violet looked down without blinking. "That's about when I lost the twins."

"So this letter must've come right after it happened."

Violet snatched the letter, quickly reading it.

Dear Tristan,

This is not my news to share, but I feel an obligation to tell you. Violet recently miscarried twins. She believes you were the father because you two were in a relationship until recently. She is hurting immensely right now. I think she'd appreciate hearing from you, but if you choose not to reach out, please at least pray for her.

The handwriting looked vaguely familiar. Who would've written this? On the one hand, Violet wanted to thank this mystery person, but on the other hand, this person was correct in saying it wasn't his or her news to share. Because it was written in cursive, she ruled out anyone her own age or younger, which didn't exactly narrow it down.

"Do you mind if I take a picture of this?" Violet pulled her phone out of her pocket. Maybe if she had more time to study the handwriting, she could figure out who wrote it. Then again, what would it change? It wouldn't bring the twins back.

"Please, go ahead."

Violet took a few photos from different angles. "I just don't get it. Why didn't you ever say anything to me?"

"Sadie…"

"No, don't blame Sadie. You could've reached out to her and asked her to pass along a message or tell her that you knew about the twins at least and you wanted to talk to me!"

Tristan leaned closer into the table. "I guess I didn't think you wanted to hear from me. I thought it would make things worse. There was nothing I could do at that point to change anything."

Violet rolled her eyes. "What a convenient excuse! I think you were a coward, and you're grateful Sadie told you to stay away from me because then you didn't have to man up." Violet sulked back in her chair.

"Violet, believe me when I say I wanted to be there for you. If I could go back and change it all, I would. I'm sorry. I'm so, so sorry."

She felt tears sprouting from the inner crevices of her eyes. Did she believe him? It was easy for him to say all the right words now, but he had no actions to back it up. All this time, she hemmed and hawed over whether to tell Tristan, and he already knew! She clenched her fists. Not only had she lost the twins, but she'd lost years of peace holding on to a secret that wasn't even secret.

"I want to make it up to you. I assume you had a lot of medical bills for the twins' care, so I'd like to reimburse you for those expenses."

Why did he have to offer his support at a time like this? No amount of money could capture what she'd lost. Just a couple of years ago, she had paid her last installment on her last payment plan. A part of her wanted to seem fine and self-reliant and say, "I don't need your money," but a bigger part of her appreciated it. She had depleted all of her savings and was rebuilding it now.

"But you're a priest now. You don't make much."

"That's true, but I made a lot before becoming a priest, so it's all in savings."

Violet nodded, not wanting to appear overly excited at the idea of some financial support. What would Jude think? They were engaged now, and pretty soon, all of his money would be hers and vice versa. She knew she was in good hands. "I appreciate the offer, but I would rather you make the equivalent donation to Sister Maria's crisis pregnancy center. It was really helpful for me."

"I can do that."

"Good." Violet nodded, telling herself to hold back tears until she went outside. "Alright, I think we're done here." Her forehead tingled as if it would splinter into a million pieces. She stood up, pushed in her chair, and walked out.

* * * * *

"So he found out from some mysterious note? Why would he believe that and not follow up?" Sadie asked as she drove Violet back to their bungalow.

"He said he didn't follow up because if it was true, what could he do?"

"That's a cop out!"

"I agree. He absolutely should have reached out or checked with you about how I was doing, at least."

"Maybe I shouldn't have told him to stay away from you," Sadie said. "Then, maybe you could've gotten the closure you needed. We didn't know about the twins when I told him to stay away."

"Sadie, look, I don't blame you, at all," Violet said. "It probably was best that Tristan never reached out to me. Who knows how my life might have changed?"

"I don't even want to think about it. Praise God that didn't happen."

Violet stopped for a second. "Maybe I never would have met Jude. Or maybe I would have tried to make it work with Tristan again. We probably would have bonded over the death of the twins. Who knows? Maybe he wouldn't have become a priest."

Sadie laughed. "You're joking, right?"

"It's interesting to consider the possibilities. What could've been."

Sadie pulled into their driveway. "Vi, you realize that you're getting married in a few months to Jude. Remember him? Why would you even think another second about trashy Tristan?" She and Sadie trudged through the snow to their front door.

She reluctantly laughed at Sadie's nickname for Tristan. Her protectiveness defaulted to insults. "Relax. Everyone thinks of their ex from one time or another." *Right?*

"Sure, but your ex is a leech who brought nothing but strife to your life," Sadie said. "And that rhymed, which must mean it's true."

"Ok, Sadie, I get it. You don't like him," Violet sighed. "By the way, do you remember where we put those brown boxes when we moved in?"

"You're going to have to be more specific."

"The brown boxes from Mom's house with all of our stuff from growing up. She labeled each one."

Sadie scrunched her nose. "I think they're in the crawl space upstairs in my bedroom. Why?"

"Tristan let me take a photo of the letter, and I think I know who wrote it, but I need to find another letter to double-check the handwriting."

"And are you going to leave me in suspense until you figure it out?"

"Of course," Violet smirked. "What fun would it be if I just told you right now?"

Sadie grunted and rolled her eyes. "You're not even going to give your getaway driver a hint?"

Chapter 14

———●———

"I'm shocked he knew and never said anything." Jude flipped each of the grilled cheese sandwiches on the griddle at his apartment. "That's weak."

Violet groaned. "Transparency has never been his strong point."

"What were his reasons for not reaching out?"

Violet summarized their conversation, including the no-contact edict from Sadie. "I've been beating myself up all these years for not telling him, and lo and behold, he already knew."

"I don't know Tristan at all, but it sounds like a lame excuse to me. I guess it's nice that he offered to pay you back for all the medical stuff."

"Yea, let's see whether he actually follows through and makes the donation to the pregnancy center." She opened the fridge and shifted some bottles and containers around. "Where's the ketchup?"

"It should be on the shelf in the door. Can you grab the mustard and relish, too?"

"Will you ever grow out of liking that odd combination?"

"Probably not. You should try it sometime."

She reached up and squeezed his shoulder. "You say that every time."

"One of these times, you'll listen to me." He bent down and kissed her. Violet smiled and basked in the warmth of his touch.

Turning back to food preparation, she squirted a pool of ketchup on her plate and the mustard-relish combination on his and then filled a bowl with salt and vinegar chips.

"Here's the other thing," she said between munching on the chips and licking her fingers. "I'm ninety-nine percent sure Sister Maria wrote that letter to Tristan. I found a letter she wrote to me, and I compared it to the picture of the letter I took. It looks almost identical."

She rummaged through her laptop bag to find the note. "Here, take a look." She held the old letter up. It was on a beautiful pink sheet of paper with Sister Maria's letterhead. "Now, look at the letter Tristan received." She scrolled to the picture on her phone.

"Wow, Vi, I think you're right." He turned back to the grilled cheeses and used the spatula to shovel each one onto their plates.

"I wonder why she told him secretly," Violet pondered.

"She probably wasn't allowed to. Isn't she bound by confidentiality to not disclose your medical history?"

"Yea, I guess so. I'm not mad at her. I'm just curious about the whole situation because I've talked to her about how conflicted I felt about telling him."

They sat down across from each other at the round table. "She probably felt guilty knowing the truth and he didn't."

"Good point," Violet said.

"You still talk to her, don't you? Why don't you just ask?"

Violet shrugged. "I don't want to make her feel bad, though." She shook her head. "Enough serious talk! I want to eat and relax."

They said grace and dug into their lunch.

"This is so good!" Violet squealed.

"I'm glad I can make you happy with something as simple as a grilled cheese."

"You make me happy just by being you."

"We'll see if you still say that in ten years," Jude teased.

"Why don't we start planning the honeymoon?"

Jude took a long sip of his iced tea and cleared his throat. His demeanor changed. "Ehh, I'm not really in a rush. We have…what?…five months to plan it."

"I think it's one of the most fun parts of all of this. Just think, you and me on an island with no one to bother us! It'll be amazing."

Jude shrugged, with a blank stare.

"What's wrong?" Violet put down her grilled cheese. "I can tell something is on your mind." Her heartbeat picked up a little. Was he having second thoughts?

"Nothing."

"It's not nothing," she prodded.

Jude huffed. "Vi, please stop with the detective skills. Everything is fine."

Her temperature rose. What was going on? "What just happened? I feel like we were having fun, and all of a sudden you're in a slump. Did I say something?"

"No." He shook his head.

"If you say so." Something was off, and she could tell that his mind was elsewhere. She mentally replayed their conversation. When she mentioned the honeymoon, he flinched and clammed up. Through bites of crispy grilled cheese dipped in ketchup, she tried to calm down, reminding herself that Jude loved her. Maybe he just wasn't in the mood to plan a vacation. But that wasn't like him. He loved to travel. Why did everything with men need to be so complicated? She couldn't shake the nagging pit in her stomach that something bothered him and he wouldn't talk about it. Did it have to do with their relationship? And why couldn't Jude be honest? She thought they were closer than this.

She decided to change the subject and sound chipper. "I'm going on that retreat my mom bought me this weekend."

"Nice." She detected that he also feigned enthusiasm.

"I'll be there for Mass and lunch on Sunday, so we won't be able to do our usual church and brunch." Violet frowned, hoping Jude was disappointed, too.

Chapter 15

———— •◆• ————

On Friday night, Violet pulled into the parking lot of the Marie Joseph Spiritual Center in Biddeford. It was just past six, but the sun had already set. She'd have to wait until morning to see the Atlantic coastline she had admired from the photos on the center's website. The center had been converted from an old white hotel perched on the beach.

When she checked in, a short nun with twinkling hazel eyes passed Violet her room key. "It's so nice to see a young person here."

Violet smiled. "My mom bought me this retreat as a wedding gift."

"Oh! How lovely! When are you getting married?"

"Five months and eight days." Violet smiled. *That is, if Jude still wants to marry me after his odd behavior the other night.*

"We'll keep you in our prayers," the nun said genuinely.

"Thank you."

"Dinner is being served now. I can show you the way. Actually, one more thing…did you happen to sign up for spiritual direction for the weekend?" the sister asked.

"I did."

The sister moistened her finger and thumbed through a few pages until she found Violet's name. "Excellent. Your first session is tomorrow morning at 9 after prayer and breakfast. You can meet Father in the office on the first floor, next to the library."

Violet smiled. "I'll be there."

"No need to bring your bags to the room now, if you'd rather wait until after dinner."

"Can you tell I'm hungry?" Violet asked.

"No one goes hungry at the Marie Joseph Spiritual Center."

* * * * *

Violet woke to the sound of the Atlantic Ocean waves rushing onto the sand. Her eyes readjusted to the light. Without her phone, she didn't know the time, so she threw on a sweater dress and headed downstairs. It was 8:48 a.m. She'd missed morning prayer and had just a few minutes left for breakfast. She couldn't remember the last time she'd slept in this late, but she felt "fresh as a daisy," as Grandma used to say.

Violet topped her plate with pancakes and home fries and grabbed a glass of orange juice. She slipped into a seat at a table with other retreatants and smiled at each of them, thankful that the silence meant she wouldn't have to make small talk.

After she rushed through her breakfast in five minutes, one of the sisters walked over to Violet as she placed her plate in the dirty dish pile.

"Father is running just a couple of minutes late, but you can wait inside the office. Follow me." She unlocked the door and turned on the lights. "He'll be here shortly."

Violet walked into the small study. "No problem."

The room's window overlooked the front side of the retreat center, a view absent from the tempting waves of the ocean. It was probably better that way. How could one work on spreadsheets or payroll when the beach was calling? She cozied onto the couch, feeling like she was about to start a therapy session. She turned her head when she heard heavier footsteps enter.

Father Tristan? This had to be *another* joke.

"You're the spiritual director here?" A part of Violet was intrigued.

Father Tristan laughed and shook his head. "I am this weekend. Trust me, this was not planned." He settled into a chair opposite Violet.

"Is there someone else I can talk to for spiritual direction this weekend? Maybe one of the sisters?"

"Yes, of course. Let me go check on that," he said, rising from his seat.

"Wait," Violet heard herself say. "I don't want to mess up the schedule for anyone. This is fine. I just don't understand how this keeps happening. You and me." *Ugh. Why did I say that? I should've just let him grab one of the sisters.*

"Me neither," he said, sitting back down. "But I'm going to take it as a sign from the Lord that maybe we should talk. It seems like, without either of us trying, we're ending up in the same place at the same time fairly often."

Violet shook her head. "Of course, you're going to say this is divinely inspired." *Settle down. Try to be more charitable. He doesn't need to see the negative impact he's had on you.*

"So you don't think so?"

"I think that we both live in the same general area of Maine, and we're both Catholic. I go to church, and you're a priest, so I think the chances are pretty good that we would cross paths at some point."

"Ok. Let's go with that. If we're going to keep running into each other, then I think we need to clear the air."

"And what does that look like?" Violet folded her arms across her chest.

"For starters, things got tense the other day at the coffee shop, and I don't feel like we ended on a good note."

Violet groaned. "But that's completely understandable, given our history. I can't just forget everything. We'll never escape the fact that we almost had a family together. That's not just casual stuff."

"No, it's not. Also, can you keep your voice down? These walls are old and thin, and I don't want to cause a scandal."

"You did always care about how others thought of you. Plus, all of this happened before you were in seminary."

"It wouldn't change my status, but I think it would be a bit of a black cloud."

"Well, that's a shame," Violet said. "If parishioners can't look past it, it's their loss. Aren't we supposed to be forgiving, understanding, and not cast the first stone and all that?"

"Yes, but a lot of people think priests don't have feelings and don't face temptation. It's a lot to live up to."

She'd never considered the pressure priests were under. "You know, I thought the same thing about priests being perfect until I found out you became one. Then I realized they're all as flawed as the rest of us."

"C'mon, was I really that bad?" Tristan asked.

She raised her eyebrows.

"How about this? Forget that I'm a priest, and just say whatever is on your mind about me."

Where to even start? Over the years, she thought about what she'd say to him if she had the chance. She'd written him half a dozen letters on a yellow legal pad, all of which she then shredded. Yet, she scrambled to put together a sentence and told herself to take a deep breath. "For one, I think you're two-faced. Seven years ago, you were a self-aggrandizing womanizer who got drunk multiple times a week and was known for falling down the stairs at the pub on several occasions."

He nodded his head. "All truth."

"And then, of all things, you're a priest now! You have to be celibate now, which apparently was not an option for you when we dated. You just *had* to have sex with me. You said you wouldn't wait until marriage, and that was the condition of our relationship. No sex, no exclusivity. I had next to no self-respect then, so I just let you pressure me for months until I relented." Violet pouted, thinking back on the three occasions they had gotten physical. One of them had led to the conception of the twins.

Tristan went from nodding his head without blinking to chomping on his lip. His cheeks were starting to resemble the shade of a red delicious apple.

"You know what, the sex wasn't even enjoyable. It was horrible." That would stick it to his ego. "It was physically painful, which I guess is par for the course the first few times. But that really wasn't the problem. The problem was that I didn't feel loved or cherished. You used me. You didn't care about my feelings. I told you so many times that I was saving myself for marriage, and then I just let you walk all over me." She tried to keep her nascent tears from falling, but she couldn't keep her lips from trembling. She never thought she'd have the chance to say all of this to Tristan.

He shut his eyes, breathed deeply, and then reopened them. He rubbed his temples and then looked straight at her. "I'm sorry," he said. "I could sit here and tell you how I've changed and how disgusted I am with how I acted, but I know that it won't change your experience."

She didn't want to let him off the hook just because he'd uttered two simple words.

"If you feel so bad, then why didn't you ever reach out to see how I was? Or to apologize?"

"Sadie asked me—" he started.

She held up her hand. "Tristan, that is a lame excuse, and you know it. Since when did you follow the rules? Am I supposed to believe that you didn't respect my physical boundaries for the entire time that we dated, and then all of a sudden, my sister asks you to leave me alone and you obey?"

He shook his head. "I haven't figured that part out, either. Sadie is...more intimidating than you."

"Did you just insult my sister? When are you going to learn? Have you done any reflection on our relationship?" She couldn't believe she was talking to a priest this way, but he wasn't really Father Tristan to her. She had never actually addressed him as Father, and he hadn't corrected her.

"Of course. Of course, I have." He was emphatic. "I couldn't go through seminary without facing a lot of my demons. I don't know what compelled me to heed Sadie's advice to stay away from you, but I think it was the right choice. How can I make it up to you?"

"What do you mean?" She scowled. "Are you going to magically give me my virginity and my twins back?"

"What can I do so that you don't recoil each time you see me or worry that you'll run into me?"

"There's nothing you need to do because I can choose how I react to your presence. Obviously, I wasn't expecting you to be here, so I wasn't mentally prepared."

"It sounds like you've been in therapy."

"I have, and I'm not ashamed of it. Maybe you should consider it." *Shoot, did I really just say that? I'm on a roll.*

"I'm sorry. I wasn't implying there was anything wrong with it. I just think it's a really mature response."

Did she want to accept his apology? Part of her wanted to hold on to the anger because it felt like a source of justice for the twins. She looked out the window, hoping to catch a glimpse of the clock and the time. It was silent until they both started talking at the same time.

"Sorry, you go," he said.

"No, you," she said, curious.

"I was just going to say that I know none of this was planned, you know, running into each other, but I'm enjoying the chance to talk to you. I've never forgiven myself for how things ended."

"I find that hard to believe. Come on, you give confessions. Of anyone, you know the power of it. I imagine you've confessed your sins multiple times over."

"I have, but there's still regret. I don't know if you knew, but my mother died three years ago," he said.

Her eyes widened, and a seed of compassion planted in her heart. "I…had no idea. I'm sorry."

"Thanks. The reason I'm telling you is that, as you know, she and I rarely talked as it was. But when I learned about our babies and how they passed, I reached out to her. We had a rekindling of sorts and she felt a sense of hope, in a weird way. Anyway, she still struggled with her alcoholism up until she died, but the idea that I was almost a dad really brought us closer."

"That's nice," Violet said. "Really, I'm happy to hear that you had some sense of closure with her."

"Me too. My point is that…it's had a big impact on me. I don't say that to minimize anything you've gone through because I'm sure it was so much worse, but I didn't want you thinking that I just heard the news and went on with my life like nothing happened."

She swallowed and inhaled deeply. She wished this room had a view of the ocean to help calm her down. "I figured out who wrote you that letter about the twins."

"You did?"

She nodded. "If this woman wasn't one of the sweetest nuns on the planet, I probably would've wrung her neck for telling you, but she did the right thing. She knew I wasn't going to tell you after the miscarriage."

"Was it Sister Maria?"

She broke into her first smile since she had sat down. "Good ole Sister Maria."

"I remember the night she introduced us at Theology on Tap. Do you remember that?"

"Of course," Violet laughed. "It's crazy that it was almost eight years ago."

She felt an urge to hug Tristan. It was a strange sensation to want a small taste of the past and relive the night they met when they were so full of hope and couldn't stop talking. And for the love of God, did he have to keep working out? Violet was sure she wasn't the only woman distracted by it.

"I'm curious about something, though," she said.

Someone knocked at the door. "Hold that thought." He got up and cracked open the door.

"Hi Sister, is everything alright?"

"Oh yes, Father," the woman answered. "I just wanted to keep you on schedule. Your next retreatant is ready whenever you are."

"Thank you, Sister. I'll be right out." He quietly shut the door and returned to his seat.

"Did you plan that interruption to avoid my question?" Violet laughed.

"No, I'm not that close with the big Man upstairs." He smiled. *Why did he have to do that and look all cute?* It was disarming.

"So what were you going to ask me?" he inquired.

"I think your answer will take more time than we have here," she said. "I think I have one more of these sessions tomorrow?" Her heart leapt at the idea. *Something is wrong with me if I'm excited to see my ex, who is a priest, again.*

"Yes, same time."

"I'll see you then." She rose from her chair.

"Sounds good. I think I know what you're going to ask me. Can I guess?"

"No, you'll have to wait and see." She turned immediately around, strode to the door, and walked out. She grinned as she bounded back to her room, thinking about how she'd teased him at the end of the session. Did that count as flirting with a priest? Was that leading him on?

And what about Jude? *Shit.* She didn't want to flirt with anybody. She hadn't intended to, but there was something about making Tristan squirm in his seat that brought her satisfaction. Should she skip the spiritual direction session the next morning instead? The whole point of this retreat was to enjoy silence and reflection. As usual, Tristan threw a wrench into her plans. Now, instead of focusing on prayer and quiet time, she fixated on their upcoming conversation. Could it finally be their last? Was that what she wanted?

* * * * *

"You look rested," Tristan said the next morning when Violet walked into his office. He took a sip from his "Best Priest Ever" mug. If he was anything like when they'd dated, he must be drinking black coffee.

"Thank you," Violet said. "Don't tell me you bought yourself that mug." There she was teasing him again.

"It sounds like you wouldn't be surprised if I had," he said.

"Maybe I wouldn't."

"One of my parishioners got it for me on my birthday last year." He took another sip.

She nodded. How was she supposed to segue the conversation now? Pepper him with questions? Seem interested in his life? "So, yesterday, I was going to ask you the million-dollar question."

"What's that?" he asked.

Violet swore there was a twinkle in his eye. "How in the world did you decide to become a priest?"

"Ah, great question." He nodded his head a few times, clearly in no rush.

"Did you guess my question correctly, as you said you would yesterday?" she asked.

"No, I did not, actually. I'll admit that."

Violet shifted in her seat. "What did you think I was going to ask you?"

"Hold up, now," he said. "One question at a time. I'll answer your first one, and then we can get into the second."

"Fine." Was he teasing now, too?

Tristan took another sip of his coffee and then placed the mug on the desk. "Where do I start? So, as I mentioned yesterday, my mom and I sort of reunited after you lost the twins."

Our twins.

"One of the things she requested I do with her was attend church on Sundays. That was our standing date. No matter what happened during the week, I knew I'd see her on Sunday at 10 a.m. Mass, and we'd eat brunch afterward. Don't ask me how she found her way back to the faith, but she did. It was the strangest thing. I never thought I'd live to see the day."

"Your dad must've been happy." She remembered the soft-spoken man. Meeting Skip made her even more curious as to how Tristan had become a playboy. The apple had fallen very far from the tree, indeed.

"Absolutely. As much as my mom hurt me and him, my dad wanted me to have a loving relationship with her, and he wanted her to be happy. You know, he never divorced her.

He considered her his wife until the day she died, and that was a good fifteen years after she'd moved out for good."

"Wow. How's he doing, by the way?"

"Pretty good. He's still living in the house where I grew up. He's dating and still working like a dog, but he loves his work."

"Good for him."

"I'm happy to see him happy," he said. "So, as I was saying, I started seeing the same people each week at church."

"Wait, which parish did you go to?"

"Saint Mary's," he said.

"Ok. Sorry, continue." Violet waved him on.

"You see the same people every week, you know how it is. You get to know each other. I got set up on a few blind dates with some of my mom's friends' daughters. Nothing really clicked." Was that because he was hung up on her? Tristan coughed into his elbow.

"And then, a visiting priest came one weekend," he continued. "He gave a homily about vocations. My mom asked me afterward if I had ever thought about becoming a priest. I laughed, of course. She was concerned that I was already thirty-one with no wife in sight, but plenty of failed relationships. She made some joke about how it might help reduce her days in purgatory if I were to become a priest."

"Based on what you've told me about her, that sounds like something she would say."

"Yea." He laughed, rubbing his chin. He looked off to the right for a beat. "So where was I?"

"Your mom joked about you becoming a priest."

"Right. So I brushed off her suggestion, but I was enjoying going to Mass. I'd slip in a weekday Mass here and there. Work became really stressful, so my mom bought me a retreat weekend. I didn't know—and she claims she didn't know—that it was actually a men's priestly discernment retreat."

Violet's mouth gaped. "No way!"

"I was pretty confused when I arrived. But by the end of the weekend, I was interested in it enough that I visited Saint John's Seminary. The rest, as they say, is history."

She rolled her eyes. "I hate that expression."

"Why?"

"First of all, it's trite. But, what really bugs me is that it oversimplifies people's stories. It's like you gloss over all the good parts. Am I supposed to believe that you entered seminary and lived happily ever after?"

"Yes."

She raised her eyebrows. "You have to admit. Your story is a little...suspect."

"How so?"

"Let me be blunt. You were sex-crazed, and now you're celibate. Something doesn't add up."

"I didn't say this life was easy," Tristan said. "Celibacy is difficult. You don't just lose your desires when you become a priest."

"Mmm."

"Mmm?" His eyes questioned her reaction.

"Yea, when I don't know what to say, I just mmm."

"Mmm," he imitated.

"Gosh, you really are just as much of a pill as ever. I thought seminary would've softened you."

"It has." He patted his nonexistent belly. It was probably a ploy to draw attention to his six-pack abs.

"Alright, then. What did you think I was going to ask?" She suspected it had to do with their relationship, but were they heading into dangerous territory? How would Jude feel if he knew they were rehashing the details of their past? What was the point anyway? He was a priest now, which was a permanent decision, as far as she knew. Maybe that's why it was so tempting. They both knew nothing would, or could, come of it.

Tristan cleared his throat again and took another sip of coffee. "Ok." He pursed his lips. "I thought you were going to ask me about us."

"Us?"

Tristan shrugged. "Yea, you and me, about our relationship. Why it didn't work out."

Violet felt her cheeks warm. *Us.* "Why would I ask about that? It doesn't even matter." *Did that sound convincing?*

"That's true. It just seemed like we left things unsettled back then, and I figured you had some questions."

"Well, I don't," she lied.

"Great, then. Mazel tov!"

She wasn't buying his enthusiasm. He was probably dying to ask her a question or two. She let him squirm for a minute. She started to lift herself from the couch, hoping he'd stop her. "Alright, well I think that wraps it up. I'll let you get to the people who are actually here for spiritual direction."

"Violet, can I ask you something?"

She lowered herself back onto the couch.

"What do you think happened between us?" he asked.

She held Tristan's gaze for a moment as her heart accelerated. *No, no, no.* She was not going down this road. He had invaded her thoughts for long enough.

"We just weren't right for each other." She shrugged. She wanted him to want more detail. All those years ago, she'd been the one trying to win his affection and commitment. She was the one who texted or initiated contact. She was the one who made date suggestions. She was the one who phoned him just to ask about his day.

But Tristan? He called only at night, after dark, when he felt lonely and wanted some company. He didn't commit to Friday or Saturday night dates with her, but she knew that if he wanted some action, he'd call and say he missed her and wanted to see her right away.

"Do you really believe that we weren't right for each other?" he asked.

"I think that there are multiple people with whom each of us could marry and be happy, and I think God lets us choose that person."

"You chose Jude."

Violet smiled. "He and I chose each other. You and I dated so long ago. You clearly weren't ready for a relationship, and we had different values at the time."

Tristan shifted in his chair and winced. "Violet, I have to be honest. I've never forgiven myself for how I treated you.

In some ways, I think I ran away to the priesthood. It was an easy way out."

"I'm sure it wasn't easy."

"It was easier than reflecting back on everything and changing myself for a woman," Tristan said. "I avoided all of the messiness of a romantic relationship by choosing this life."

"What are you saying?"

"I'm saying I was scared."

"Do you think you made the wrong choice?" she asked. *Shoot, was that question too much?*

Tristan hesitated. "I don't know."

He doesn't know if he made the right decision? Does he wish he had gotten married? *Is he implying that he wanted to end up with me?* Violet stuttered and pointed to the clock. "I think our thirty minutes is up. There's probably someone else waiting for you."

Tristan shook his head. "Right, of course."

This time, instead of beaming back to her room, she tread slowly. She replayed the details to piece together what happened. If he felt like he had made a mistake by becoming a priest, did that mean she was about to make a mistake, too, by marrying Jude? She groaned and flopped onto her bed. This was supposed to be a relaxing weekend, and now she felt worse than when she had arrived.

Chapter 16

Violet swirled her spoon in her cereal. The milk turned pink as the Lucky Charms shed their coloring. She'd driven to Jude's after the retreat ended early afternoon. Bedtime was just a few hours away at this point. Both tired of cooking and takeout, it was a sugary-cereal-for-dinner night.

"It's crazy that Father Tristan was there," Jude said. "That must've been weird."

"It was, and we didn't even do a typical spiritual direction session. It was more of me just airing all of my grievances against him."

"How'd he take it?" Jude took a seat across from Violet at the kitchen table with his own bowl of Honeycombs and a glass of orange juice.

Violet sighed. "He took it and didn't make excuses. But he did say something cryptic at the end."

Jude looked up from his cereal. "Yea?"

Violet stared back down into her bowl of soggy marshmallow charms. "Basically he said he ran to the priesthood out of fear because he didn't want to face his demons and change himself to be with another woman. He felt like it was the easy way out."

"I'm not sure most people would agree that the priesthood is the easy way out."

"That's what I said! And then I asked him if he thought he made a mistake with choosing that life, and he said he didn't know."

"And that was it?"

Is it necessary to mention that we flirted a bit? Wasn't flirting subjective? "Yea, our time was up, so I got up and left."

Jude put his spoon down and finished chewing. "Vi, I don't know. It sounds like he still has feelings for you."

How could she downplay it when she suspected the same thing? "I doubt it."

"Regardless, honestly, I'm not that comfortable with the two of you having alone time."

"I'm not planning to accidentally run into him again. This weekend, it wasn't my choice to see him, just so you know." Though, technically, she could've accepted Tristan's offer to speak with a nun instead or chosen not to attend her second session with him.

"I get that, but I'm just saying that moving forward, I would feel better knowing that you two aren't alone. He knows about the twins."

"I get it," she said. "I wouldn't want you hanging with an ex-girlfriend, even if she were a nun."

Jude laughed. "Ha! I can assure you that none of my ex-girlfriends are on that track."

"I would've said the same thing about Tristan, but here he is."

He reached for Violet's hand. "I want you to know, I have nothing against him. I actually really feel for him. If he's truly struggling with his decision, it must be very stressful. We should pray for him."

Violet's body relaxed at the thought. "I think that's a great idea." Maybe this was the closure she needed. Tristan knew about the twins, and she was engaged. There was nothing left to discuss. She exhaled and focused on the man next to her.

* * * * *

Sadie curled her hair in the bathroom while simultaneously applying make-up during the three-second intervals for each curl to set. It was time for final exams. Though her only audience was the faculty, Violet knew Sadie wanted to look fabulous while she presented her semester's piece.

"As usual, you're in your head way too much," Sadie yelled to Violet, who laid on her bed. "So what if you had that second session with Fake Father Tristan? That's not cheating."

"I know, but it felt indulgent. We were flirting, I think."

"Ok, then tell Jude if you're so upset about it. You always said honesty is a quality you highly value." Violet heard Sadie smack her lips together to set her red lipstick "He's a reasonable person, and I'm sure he'd understand."

"I already told him, sort of. I didn't say we were flirting, though."

"Then, I guess you'll have to revisit that conversation."

Violet screamed into a pillow. It felt immature but also satisfying. "He doesn't want me to be alone with Father Tristan anymore."

"So? What's the big deal? Why would you need to be alone with him?"

"True, but it just feels controlling."

"People say...mother of pearl!" Sadie screamed. "That damn curling wand. Now it looks like I have a hickey on my neck."

"You ok?" Violet asked, not wanting to move but fulfilling her sisterly duty to make sure Sadie was alright.

"Yea. It just looks like some guy mauled me."

"Use some concealer."

"It'll be fine. Ok, so as I was saying, people often feel controlled when they're told not to do something that they actually want to do."

"Huh?"

"If Jude told you he didn't want you smoking cigarettes, you wouldn't feel controlled because you don't care about smoking. You don't think about it."

"What's your point?"

"Violet, admit it. You want some alone time with Phony Father Tristan. You like his company. He's hot. Heck, if I didn't know about how he treated you, I'd probably want to hang out with him, too."

Violet didn't know how to respond. Was Sadie right?

"Jude didn't forbid you from hanging out with him," Sadie continued. "He just said that it would make him uncomfortable. So it's really up to you. You could hang with him and make your amazing fiancé uneasy, or you could leave the past in the past and not mess up your future. I don't know why this is so difficult for you."

Violet groaned. "I didn't realize you were studying psychology at school."

"Violet, now you're deflecting. Seriously, think about what I'm saying. There's some real gold here."

But she didn't want to think about it. If a neurosurgeon could just please remove any memory of Tristan from her head, she'd sign up for it. Why did she want to spend time with him? She had Jude. Was she crazy? So much for closure.

Chapter 17

Father Tristan bowed his head to rest on his clasped hands. His elbows rested on the pew in front of him. The adoration chapel was the quietest place he could find during the morning rush hour.

In the name of the Father, and of the Son, and of the Holy Spirit. Amen. Dear Lord, I don't know what I want to happen today with Violet, but I want to do your will. It's just not clear to me. I feel this heaviness in my heart. I hurt her immensely, and I feel like there's no way to make it up to her. It seems like she's forgiven me, thankfully. But I wonder if I should have made different choices. You know, should I have approached her years ago and made amends? I know I can't change the past, but if there's still a chance that she thinks about what we could have been, I want to know. I know I've chosen my vocation as a priest already. I'm not saying that I want to leave the priesthood. I'm confused, though. Why would I have such strong feelings for Violet when I can't act on them? Why have you allowed her back in my life? It feels like a tease. Why couldn't this have happened before my ordination? It was only just over a year ago. I guess timing is everything. Yet, I can't ignore this desire to love her, protect her, and take care of her. I know I can't do both. I can't be with Violet and be a priest. This feels torturous. I don't know what to do. Lord God, Prince of Peace, show me the way. Amen.

He blessed himself and left the chapel, asking for the intercession of Our Lady to remain with him throughout the day. He didn't know exactly what he'd say to Violet, but he needed to know if she felt the same. Had she fantasized about a future life for the two of them?

* * * * *

"It was a dramatic way to end our conversation, you're right," Father Tristan said to Violet. She giggled. He couldn't believe she'd agreed to meet him for coffee. She was about to get married, after all. He hoped she hadn't read into his cryptic statement at the end of their spiritual direction session that had instead turned into their own version of The Bachelor's After the Final Rose, where ex-lovers rehash why their relationship didn't work.

Tristan wanted closure today so he wouldn't live the rest of his life as a priest wondering, "What if…" While he wasn't sure whether one coffee "meeting" would solve it, it was worth a try. Even though he hadn't received a clear answer in the chapel, he felt at peace that he'd finally been honest with the Lord about the desires of his heart. He wasn't hiding anymore.

"So why did you agree to meet me here?" Father Tristan asked.

"I think the real question is: Why did *you* invite *me?*" Violet smirked. He took it as a sign of flirtation. Gosh, she was so beautiful.

"I felt bad about how our conversation ended the other day," he said. "By the way, does Jude know you're here?"

"I didn't mention it to him, but I wasn't trying to keep it from him, either. I'll bring it up when I see him later."

Father Tristan nodded his head. "I don't want to cause any friction between you two."

"No worries there," Violet said. Tristan sensed it might not have been the whole truth but didn't press it.

"Good to hear." A part of him secretly hoped there was some flaw with Jude that made Violet think twice. As much as he wanted her to be happy, he also wanted her to desire him. Then again, another part of him thought maybe this was a good sign. If Violet was with an amazing man and she was happy, then maybe *that* was the mark of closure he was seeking.

"So, anyway," he continued, folding his hands on the table. "I felt like I caused scandal by indicating that I somehow made a mistake by becoming a priest. That wasn't what I was trying to say. I love being a priest. Hearing confessions and saying Mass is a privilege I never thought I would have, but somehow the Lord chose me." He stopped himself from adding that a part of him still longed to be with Violet and have a family with her.

Violet nodded along. "I think we can agree that the saying, 'God doesn't call the equipped; he equips the called,' rings true here."

"I will drink to that," Father Tristan said, raising a toast to no one in particular.

An awkward silence followed. There wasn't a protocol for a priest having coffee with his ex who miscarried his babies. What did Violet think of it all?

He tried to nonchalantly change the subject. "So when's the big day?"

Violet said that the wedding was just under five months away, Sadie was her maid of honor, and they were going to have a chocolate cake. But did he notice a hint of resignation in her voice?

"I'm sure Sadie will give a rousing speech."

"That she will."

"She never really cared for me, did she?"

Violet laughed. Tristan loved seeing her smile.

"That's one way to put it. You never had siblings, so it's hard to understand, but she's very protective. I'm glad she told you to stay away. That was best."

"Do you still think so?" *Please say no.*

"Absolutely. It would've been unhealthy for us to keep trying to make our relationship work. You needed help. I needed to grow."

"You're right." *So maybe she's not feeling the same regret about how things ended with us?* He cleared his throat.

"You know how people say God can pull good out of any situation?" she asked. "If someone gave me the choice, I never would've chosen what happened. I would have walked away from you the moment you told me that we had to have sex for us to be exclusive, but I didn't. The good that God brought from that was the twins. Then, of course, losing the twins…the good that God brought from that was…I don't know. Well, maybe I wouldn't have met Jude. The amazing thing is that he totally understands what I went through."

"How so?"

"I don't think he'd mind if I share this with you, but about three years ago, before he and I met, he wasn't even a Christian. He was raised as an atheist. His parents converted to Catholicism when he was in college, but he was away at school and didn't have the same conversion experience until later. Anyway, he dated a girl, and she got pregnant and lost the baby, too."

"That's crazy that you two share that experience." He thumbed his coffee mug and bit his lip.

"It instantly made me feel comfortable because he understood a pain that so few people talk about. I could see God's hand in it. Obviously, neither one of us would've chosen a miscarriage, but God squeezed this goodness out of it by bringing us together to understand each other in a deeper way."

"That's a really beautiful way to look at it." A stab of jealousy wrenched his gut; Violet and Jude bonded over something he should have shared with her.

"If there's something I've learned in the last eight years, it's that I can wallow in my self-pity and help no one, or I can acknowledge my pain, deal with it, and let something useful come with it. It's like a compost bin. Lots of sludge creates rich soil."

Tristan smiled. "That's a great analogy. Maybe I'll steal it for one of my homilies."

Violet laughed. "As long as you give me credit."

"Then it wouldn't be stealing."

"Touché."

His face warmed. Could she tell he was blushing? Or that his heart sang? "I wondered how you were doing all these years, and it brings me peace to know that you're happy and I didn't ruin your life."

She chuckled again. "No, you didn't ruin my life in the least, and clearly, I didn't ruin yours."

Tristan fixed his gaze on Violet. "It would've been hard for any woman to compare after you."

She tilted her head and furrowed her brow. Had he said too much? He cleared his throat. "I mean, from the perspective that it's hard to come after someone who carried your children."

She nodded weakly, as if energy started to drain from her.

"It's fine. I understand what you're trying to say. I worried that no one would want to date me with all my baggage. I was horrified to tell Jude, but it turned out better than I expected." She pushed her engagement ring up and down her finger. "I actually need to get going."

Was fifteen minutes really up already?

"Can I walk you to your car?" *C'mon Tristan, really?*

She hesitated. "Uh…sure. It's no big deal, though. I'm just parked out back." She pointed.

"What would Jesus do? He'd make sure you got to your car safely."

Violet broke into a smile. "Hard to argue with that."

He led Violet out, brushing the small of her back. Was that too much? She squinted as they got outside, her crow's feet wrinkling under the gloss of the sun. He used his hand as a personal visor. "Beautiful day."

"My keys!" Violet exclaimed as they neared the car. She patted her pockets and rummaged through her purse. "I think I locked them inside!"

Was it wrong that Tristan delighted in this delay that meant they could share a few more minutes together? "Can you see them?"

"Yea, they're right there." She pointed to the driver's side floor. "They must've fallen out of my pocket when I got out of the car."

"Ok. I think we can fish them out."

"Really? How?"

"Your window is cracked open a bit. That's all I need. I'll be right back."

He ran to his car, mentally running through a list of random items he could use to retrieve her keys. He kept his car immaculate, except for a couple of empty water bottles on the passenger side floor. There was nothing to rummage through in the second row, so he checked the trunk and grabbed the only things there: two wire hangers. He felt victorious that, in a small way, he could be her hero. He sprinted back to her car.

"How is this going to work?" Violet asked as he approached.

"Just wait and see."

He tore apart one of the hangers, turning it into a long wire and then bent one end of it to act as a hook for the keys.

He pressed his body flush against the driver's side door and poked the hanger wire into the inch of space from the open window. He fished for the keys until they clung onto the hook, and he slowly pulled them out of the car.

Violet squealed. "Thank you so much!"

He dropped the keys into her hands. Her bright eyes reminded him of the joy she'd sparked in him when she made a joke or when they watched a funny movie together. How had he ever taken that for granted?

"I'm so relieved!" Her energy propelled her towards him into a hug and they held onto each other. She started to pull herself away from him but kept her eyes on his. She stopped at his elbows, letting her hands rest there.

"Violet, I..." His heart raced. Could she hear it? He didn't even know what to say, or if he was just talking to avoid temptation. As long as he talked, they weren't kissing. Did words matter at this point? He found himself gently pulling her closer and leaning his head toward hers. She didn't protest. She followed his lead. He cupped her sweet face in his hands. He'd missed her smooth hair and how it felt to run his fingers through it.

He breathed deeply. "Violet..." he closed his eyes, his voice husky. Their lips were a brush away. And then Violet pulled away quickly. She threw her hand over her mouth, her engagement ring sparkling under the sun. "Oh my gosh, what are we doing? Tristan! We can't...we shouldn't."

"Vi, I'm so sorry. You're right." *What was I thinking? How did I let myself get here?* He ran his hand through his hair and looked around to make sure no one had seen.

"I should go. Thanks again for helping me with my keys." Violet swung open her car door and threw herself in. Tristan watched her drive away, wishing he could erase the last five minutes. Either way, he'd gotten one answer: somewhere, deep inside, Violet still had feelings for him, too.

Chapter 18

Violet fidgeted in line outside the confessional the next morning. She'd opted to go to a different Catholic Church just north of Portland because she didn't want to risk confessing to Father Goren, who hopped around different parishes to fill in during Ogunquit's off-season. He was supposed to be the witness at their wedding, but would the wedding still be on after she told Jude what had happened? Her heart plunged at the thought. How could one minute possibly ruin everything? She shuffled inside when it was her turn and went through her opening words. She sighed slowly.

"This is embarrassing to admit because I love my fiancé so much. But I have a crush on someone else. It's someone who I could never be with for certain reasons." She paused.

"Have you and this man been in a near occasion of sin?" he asked tenderly and without judgement.

"Yes. Should I give details?"

"Only if you wish. It's not necessary, though."

She couldn't help but picture the priest as the sweet-looking Ernie Keebler from the cookie and cracker brand. Praise God priests couldn't read minds in confessionals! She welcomed any thoughts that were a distraction from her own self-loathing of the sin to which she was about to admit.

"Well, Father, I'd really love to describe what happened because it's weighing on me, and I haven't told anyone." How could she tell the story in a way that made her look as innocent as possible? Then again, this was a confession, so what was the point of trying to hide her behavior? She smiled to herself, thinking it silly that she often tried to paint herself in as good a light as possible in confession when Jesus already knew everything. She explained to the priest how she met up with Tristan yesterday. Was it necessary to mention fleeting moments of flirtation, or was that scrupulous?

"Anyway, at the end, we both leaned in to kiss each other, but I pulled away at the last moment when I realized how wrong it was. And that's it. I haven't talked to him since then. I'm so embarrassed that I wanted to kiss him and almost did."

Her heart sank, thinking of Jude's possible reaction.

"Are you sharing more of your heart with this man than with your fiancé?" the priest asked.

"In some ways, yes."

"It is not a sin to notice the beauty in others. You see the beauty of God's creation in this other man, your ex-boyfriend. In marriage, you won't just magically lose attraction to all other men. Being attracted to someone else doesn't mean there's something wrong with your current relationship. It doesn't mean you don't love the person you're with or that you're not supposed to be with him. In fact, not acting on that attraction shows that you love your future husband and you honor your vows."

"But I can't keep living like this, where I love one man and have feelings for another."

"It sounds like you think that because you have these feelings for an old flame, it must mean that you should have chosen to stay with him instead of your fiancé," the priest pondered.

"Yes," Violet said, relieved to finally express it without having to say the words. "Why else would God put these feelings in my heart?"

"I don't claim to know why God allows certain things. You have free will, so maybe, you can ask, 'What is God trying to teach me with these feelings?'"

"I don't know. I'd have to think about it."

"That's ok," Father said. "And it's ok if you never receive a satisfying answer. The point isn't that you get an answer from God. It's that you *seek* an answer from God. Anytime we bring our struggles or our joys to God and lay them at His feet, we grow closer to Him. That is the whole point."

Violet sighed and massaged her temples. "Father, can you give me some practical advice here? I'm really struggling. Am I crazy?"

The priest chuckled. "Of course not. I'm privy to much of the inner thoughts of our parishioners. More people than you realize have attraction to someone they're not married to. I'm not talking about a celebrity crush. I'm talking about someone in their life who they interact with. It could be a co-worker, a friend's spouse, their doctor, even the local barista." *Or their priest.*

"Wow, I'm surprised people admit that."

"How would marriage be such a commitment if one never found another attractive? The fact that a husband or a wife is attracted to someone else isn't the problem. The problem is when someone acts on it."

Violet nodded her head.

"This young man you're engaged to now—is he a loving, trustworthy man of God?"

"Absolutely."

"And you love him?"

"No question."

"Then, you have a choice. You can either feed this crush or starve it. You can either continue to straddle a line and put yourself in more near-occasions of sins, or you can cut it off completely."

Starve this crush. I need to starve this crush. I will starve this crush.

Chapter 19

———◆———

Later that day, Violet paid closer attention to the items inside Jude's apartment. She still couldn't tell whether that sad succulent on the TV stand was actually alive. She smiled at the photo montage on the wall that his sister-in-law made him from his soccer-playing days. She scanned the small selection of books, mostly non-fiction, on the tiny bookshelf his mother gave him for his "bachelor pad." Would this be the last time she'd see all that?

She closed her eyes and took a deep breath.

"Violet, you ok?" Jude came out of the bathroom drying his hands on his jeans. No matter how many times she told him to use the towel, he wouldn't. It was a trait that made her laugh and cringe at the same time, thinking of their future children not drying their hands in the bathroom, either.

"Yea, I'm good." Her voice was tremulous. She reached for the rolled arm of the couch to steady herself.

Jude rushed over. "Are you feeling alright? You look kind of pale."

"No, I'm good. I'm just a little tired."

The concern in his eyes captured her. What would those same eyes look like in two minutes when he knew everything? This was more nerve-wracking than when she told him about losing the babies. That act felt more distant because it had happened years before they knew each other. It wasn't something that Jude had to forgive. She hadn't wronged him. But this. This was precarious. She couldn't fault herself for having feelings for Tristan, but as the priest said, she was either feeding the crush or starving it. If she were honest with herself, it was more like she was bingeing.

She held her stomach as though she was pregnant. It brought her comfort to hold herself. With her other hand, she rested her forehead on her palm, holding up the remaining shreds of her dignity.

Jude sat down next to her. "I know this may not feel like the ideal time, but I want to talk to you about something."

He knew! How did he know already? Had someone seen her and Tristan in the parking lot and then relayed the scene to him?

"Ok, what is it?" she asked, certain of her fate.

He clenched his fists and then released them. He stood, started pacing the room, and patted the top of his head. "This is really hard for me to talk about."

Violet's heart galloped.

"It's about when I dated Leona."

Wait, what? Maybe this had nothing to do with Tristan. "Does this have to do with why you've been clamming up when I talk about the honeymoon?"

He nodded. "So, when I told you I understood what it was like to lose a baby, I meant it. Let me sit down, actually."

He lowered himself onto an armchair diagonally across from where she sat on the couch. What is going on? Could Jude just be out with it, already?

"There's more to what I told you about Leona's pregnancy."

"Ok." *How much more?*

His voice shook. "I can't even look at you when I say this." He covered his face with his hands.

"Leona lost the baby, yes, but not because of a miscarriage. She had an abortion, and I was the one who encouraged her to do it."

Violet scowled. *What?!*

"Vi, can you say something?"

"Oh my gosh…" Her gaze hadn't left the floor or the Persian rug and her head fell into her hands. "I can't look at you, either. This is wrong on so many levels. It's horrible what you did, and it's horrible that you lied to me."

"I know, I know." Jude started to cry for the first time in their relationship.

"You proposed to me without giving me the freedom to say yes knowing all of the facts."

"I thought you wouldn't want to be with me, and this was all before my conversion, so I thought it wouldn't matter."

"You thought it wouldn't matter to me that you had encouraged someone to take a human life? Really?"

"Of course, I thought it mattered," Jude explained. "But, when I weighed the risks, I just kept telling myself it was in the past, and it didn't change anything that we shared."

"Except that I opened up to you about my past, and you made it seem like you totally understood. That bonded us early on. We went to miscarriage support groups together." She folded her arms across her chest, still keeping her eyes glued to the carpet.

A few minutes in silence, save for Jude's sniffles as he stifled his tears, passed. She heard the hands on the clock tick, something she had never noticed before.

Jude blew his nose. "So where do we go from here? I love you and I want to be with you."

If she wanted a way out, this was it. She could leave Jude understandably and let him think it was his fault they broke up. She could walk out of here with the same result—a broken engagement—without having to confess what happened with Tristan. She wouldn't have to drag herself through the explanation and see the hurt she caused him or face the consequences for her actions. Meanwhile, she knew Jude would beat himself up. "I know you were at a much different place in your life when all of that happened…"

"And I've confessed it all, just so you know. I know God forgives me, but I haven't forgiven myself."

"Honestly, I can't imagine the anguish or regret you live with now. I wouldn't wish that feeling on anyone. But you lied. We've been together for almost a year and a half. You had plenty of opportunities to be honest with me about it, but instead you kind of tricked me into the marriage proposal." *Shoot, that was a dramatic choice of words*

He lunged forward in his chair. "Tricked you?"

Just keep going with it. "Yes. Like I said, I didn't know all the facts. I'm just grateful I knew this before we walked down the aisle."

"So what are you saying?"

Am I really about to do this? She wriggled her engagement ring on her finger and pulled it off. She walked over to Jude and placed it in his hand, cupping it shut. "I think it's best if we just leave it at that."

"Violet, please no. I love you."

She hurried out of his apartment, not feeling deceived so much as feeling like the deceiver. Her stomach lurched, and her legs wobbled beneath her. Jude was supposed to be her safe haven. It was over? Just like that? And she'd been the one to end it? Was that really what she wanted?

Violet couldn't come up with any excuses. She was wrong. She'd made a mistake. She'd gotten too close to a man who wasn't her fiancé. She'd done the equivalent of window shopping, only to enter the store, pick something out, and carry it to the cashier before turning around right before she paid.

Way to go, Violet.

Now, a part of her almost wished she had kissed Tristan. If her engagement was going to break off regardless of whether they actually kissed, she secretly wished she could have tasted

Tristan's lips just one more time. What would it be like to kiss a mature man now, instead of the infantile bachelor he'd been when they dated? Violet shook her head to empty the thought from her mind. *No, it would not have been better to kiss him*, she assured herself. *He's a priest, and I would've been cheating on my fiancé.*

She staggered to her car, running through a list of people she could reach out to for support. Sadie was at rehearsal. Sister Maria was probably asleep. She could call her mom, but she was a good two-hour drive away, and a talk with her mom may or may not involve a long conversation about sex and pregnancy, neither of which she wanted to endure. She hadn't really made any close friends at work yet. *This is pathetic.*

Violet remembered how Father Goren suggested she go to Adoration a few months back, but she couldn't remember where he said it was held. She Googled "Adoration near me" before turning the car on. It was raining hard, and she felt comfort that perhaps the whole world was crying with her. The "Cathedral of the Immaculate Conception" in Portland popped up as the closest Adoration site currently open. It wasn't exactly down the road, but it was her only hope.

Her stomach rumbled as she navigated along I-95 North. It had been hours since she'd eaten. When she saw a sign for a diner at the next exit, she turned off the main road. With her luck, Tristan would also be at this exact diner, because she was convinced God was using her life as a dark comedy for his own entertainment.

Violet pulled her hoodless jacket over her head as she tried to evade the raindrops on her way inside. She settled into a corner booth and perused the gargantuan, laminated menu. She knew what she wanted to order, but it didn't hurt to take another look at the stained, plastic pages. Whenever they went to a diner, Sadie always complained about how burgers tasted like pancakes and grilled cheese tasted like French toast. "It's all cooked on the same stove," she'd moan.

"That's the best part. Multiple flavors in one!" Violet would reply, to which Sadie would roll her eyes and order a plain baked potato with a side of fruit.

Violet smiled to herself, reveling in her solo, cozy dinner. *Not so bad.* No one could pass judgement on what she ate, she could take as long as she wanted, and best of all, no one was waiting up for her. She was free to spend her time as she wanted.

The approaching waitress reminded Violet of her grandma: frail-looking but full of pep. Violet wondered what happened in her life that led her to waitressing at a suburban family diner in her older years. Had she not saved enough to retire? Maybe she just enjoyed being around people. Violet didn't notice a ring on her finger. Had she been married? Divorced? Widowed? Did she have kids or grandkids? She knew it wasn't any of her business, but she hoped the woman went home each night to people who loved her.

She ordered breakfast for dinner: a bacon, egg, and cheese sandwich on a hard roll with a side of home fries and more crispy bacon, which she would, of course, dip into the maple syrup. Their mom used to declare "breakfast for dinner" when she or Sadie had a bad day growing up. She longed for a hug from her mom, or really anyone, right now.

"Hot and delicious," the waitress said as she placed Violet's breakfast plate in front of her.

"Thank you so much."

"You look sad, honey. Everything ok?"

Violet wondered how much she should share. "Yea, it's been a tough day." *To say the least.* She tried to hold back tears. Why was she opening up to a stranger like this in a diner? A tear rolled down her flushed cheek. She quickly wiped it away.

"Oh, sweetie." The woman sat across from Violet in the booth. "I knew something was wrong from the moment I looked at you."

Violet laughed. "I'm not good at hiding my emotions when I'm sad."

"Nothing wrong with that. Eat up, sweetie."

Violet dove in, relishing the warm sandwich and sentimental combination of cheese, bacon, and eggs.

"I'll tell the chef you love it," the waitress said.

Violet smiled. Again, she wondered about this woman's story. Not that it changed anything. She was accompanying Violet in a tough moment and that was more than anyone else right now. "I'm Violet, what's your name?"

"Renee." She settled into the booth.

"Thank you for sitting down with me, Renee. I feel like a mess."

"Happy to. This is why I love my job."

Violet licked some maple syrup off her pointer finger.

"Truth is, sweetie, I don't have to be here. I choose to be here. My husband and I are both retired, and I love the man, but I cannot be around him twenty-four seven. So I come here, and I get to talk to people like you."

Violet smiled. "I think that's great. How long have you been married?"

"Forty-seven years next month."

"Wow." Learning of this woman's long and happy marriage soothed her. Violet tried to imagine what it would feel like to know someone so intimately for so long. "What's the secret?"

"Forgiveness."

"That's interesting…I wasn't expecting you to say that."

"Yea, it's not glamorous. He's flawed. I'm flawed. It wouldn't work if we couldn't look past that and still love each other."

Violet nodded as she chewed on another piece of bacon.

"Gosh, when I think back on our wedding day, if I had been given a test of forgiveness, I would have failed. I didn't know it because I was so young, but I held a lot of grudges against a lot of people."

"But now you don't?" Violet asked. She took a sip of her orange juice.

"No, honey, I am a free woman! I just learned to forgive and let things go."

"How?"

"Lots of practice." Her gaze held memories of a haunted past. "You could talk all you want about the importance of forgiveness, but until you're put in the position to forgive someone for something that really hurt you, it's not real."

Violet wondered what Renee had to forgive. Forgiveness in marriage wasn't a new concept, but it frustrated her when people talked about it without explicitly mentioning the offending action. Were they talking about forgiveness over burning dinner on the stove? Or something more serious? Infidelity? She wouldn't press Renee on the details.

"That's an amazing journey." Violet borrowed from her reporting vocabulary. It was an open-ended statement that invited the other person to share more without overtly asking them another question.

"When you get to my age, all the years start to blend together. But by the grace of God, we're together and still healthy. I'm sorry—I don't mean to bring up God. My boss—" she signaled with her thumb to the balding, middle-aged man at the register "—tells me to keep my God talk to myself. I just saw that porcelain cross around your neck and figured it was safe."

Violet grasped her necklace. "It was my grandma's."

"Precious. My grandbabies aren't old enough to understand that yet, but when they are, I can't wait."

"Grandmas are special people." Violet wondered what Grandma would think of everything going on.

"Did your grandma pass?" Renee asked.

The muscles in Violet's neck seized. She nodded.

"You know that she loved you very much."

"I know. I was very lucky." Violet remembered all of the afternoons her grandma stood on their front porch waiting for her and Sadie as they got off the school bus. More times than not, their mom worked her shift at the hospital while Grandma made them snacks and talked to them about their day. Her Grandma's death and the break-up with Tristan had all happened in the same week. It had been too much.

"I'm getting the feeling that you weren't crying over your grandma tonight, but over a guy?"

Violet sighed. "Story of my life."

"Well, since I know you're a God-fearing woman, I can tell you to bring Him your struggles, honey. He always listens."

"Yes, but I'm afraid He's having too much fun seeing me suffer." Violet shook her head.

Renee leaned in closer. "Oh, honey. You really believe that?"

"It's hard not to," Violet said, stifling her tears.

"Suffering is a mysterious part of life. I can't say I have it all figured out, and I don't think I ever will." Renee shrugged.

"But what I do know is that he is waiting for you with open arms."

Violet nodded. "I was actually on my way to the Cathedral for Adoration."

"That's a beautiful place," she said. "My husband and I are members at the Baptist church here in town, but sometimes I go to that Cathedral for peace and quiet."

"That's exactly what I'm looking for." Violet laughed. Should she share more about her situation? Maybe Renee could offer some advice.

"Well, Miss Violet, I have to check on the other customers. I truly would love to stay and chat longer, but this diner ain't empty." Renee gave a toothy grin.

"Thanks for stopping to talk with me."

"My pleasure, honey."

Violet took out her phone after Renee walked away. "How'd it go with Jude? You coming home tonight?" Sadie's text read.

Violet rolled her eyes. She knew it was an innocent question on Sadie's part, but at this moment, having to answer for her whereabouts bothered her. Couldn't she have uninterrupted time?

"Maybe. Tell you more about Jude and me later," she texted back, thinking there was no more "Jude and me."

"I'll keep the porch light on just in case," Sadie wrote back with a kiss face emoji.

Violet took another bite of her sandwich, relishing the sweet ketchup against the smoky bacon and savory cheese. She dipped some of her home fries, too. They were lukewarm now, but she still gobbled them up. A frequent member of the Clean Plate Club, she took the last sip of her orange juice and caught Renee's eyes for another glass.

Jude hadn't texted her since she'd left, and she vowed not to be the first one to reach out. She knew it was petty and immature, but she wasn't interested in being the bigger person right now. She wanted to be the small person, the one huddling down in a pit of misery, locked in her own sadness. A pity party. She'd come out of it, but not now. For now, she would wallow in it.

She grabbed the sticky, plastic menu again, considering dessert. Chocolate cake. Carrot cake. Apple crisp. She'd also eyed a frisbee-sized chocolate chip cookie in the bakery case on her way in.

Renee returned a minute later with more orange juice. "What'll it be?" she asked.

"It's a tough call," Violet said. "I'm leaning toward that chocolate chip cookie over there."

"Can I suggest it a la mode? On the house!"

"I can't refuse that offer." Violet shut the menu and handed it back to Renee.

"I'll be right back." Renee returned a couple of minutes later with a plate all but covered by the cookie and a dish full of ice cream.

"Bon appétit," Renee said.

Violet broke the cookie in half and spread the vanilla ice cream on top, making an open-faced ice cream sandwich. She bit into it, the cool dessert falling into the craters of the crumbly cookie. Violet recalled her mom telling her not to cope with her feelings by eating, but she had to admit that this was doing the job quite well. Who was Jude anyway? And there was nothing Tristan could say that would make this dessert anything but delicious. Perhaps one day, both Jude and Tristan would mean nothing to Violet, and in retirement, like Renee, she could live in peace and work at a diner just to talk to people.

Renee came over with the bill. "No rush. You can pay Mr. Bob over at the register whenever you're ready."

"Thank you." Violet offered her a smile in gratitude.

"You remember the Big Man upstairs." Renee winked.

Chapter 20

Violet turned up Celine Dion on her car's stereo because who better than her to commiserate with over heartbreak? Celine could understand her plight. If it weren't for the rain, she'd have the windows down, her hair blowing, and the speakers blaring. The chorus called for turning up the volume. *Maybe my heart will go on, like Celine's.*

The spire of the Cathedral in Portland protruded into the dim night sky. She slowed as she approached the church, scanning for a parking spot, while the blinking traffic lights reflected off of the puddles in the street. She noticed a small lot next to the church. *Thank you, Jesus, for not making me parallel park.*

Half a dozen other cars were scattered around the lot. Violet quickly checked her hair in the rearview mirror, tousling some unruly wisps back in place. She walked up the stone steps to the towering, wooden double doors and grabbed onto the black handles.

Inside, a powerful silence enveloped her. There was a stillness, a presence that penetrated her soul. Even though it was quiet, there was life. She scanned the church to see how many others were there and picked a pew toward the back.

The lights were dimmed, and her eyes were drawn to the monstrance on the altar. *How does this work? What am I supposed to do? Is there some opening prayer I should know about?*

She fidgeted on the kneeler, observing the others. Some knelt, and some sat with their back against the pew.

In the name of the Father, and of the Son, and of the Holy Spirit. Amen. Jesus…I'm here because Father Goren suggested I come. I'm not really sure what to do.

She heard footsteps down the aisle behind her. *Oh, God. Please don't be Tristan.*

Chapter 20

It wasn't him, but it was a man, probably in his forties. He walked slowly toward the front of the church. Violet kept her eye on him, wondering why he wouldn't just pick one of the eight dozen empty pews he passed. When he got to the front of the church, he knelt down, made the sign of the cross, and dropped himself to the floor, lying prostrate.

What is he doing?

Violet looked at the other people to see if anyone else's facial expression might indicate that they, too, thought this behavior was strange. It felt like one of those moments on an airplane with crazy turbulence where you'd look around to gauge everyone else's level of panic and adjust your reaction accordingly. Not a single head lifted or cocked in the direction of this man. *It must be normal then.* Typically, she'd mentally tag it as something to ask Jude about later, but now that wasn't an option.

Ok, Jesus. Sorry about the distraction. I'm really lost here. I don't think I can forgive Jude. The Bible verse about how many times to forgive people flashed in her mind: "I do not say to you seven times, but seventy times seven" (Matthew 18:22). She did quick math: seventy times seven is four hundred and ninety times. Could she make an argument that she'd already forgiven people that many times in her life and therefore had done her part as a Christian and was now free to not forgive others?

Lord, my life is insanity. Did Jude and I really break up tonight? For a supposed man of God, he wasn't very forthcoming about the abortion. I mean, I could forgive him for that, but to lie about it? How could I trust him? I feel like he manipulated me. When we started dating, and I told him my story, he was understanding about it. Now I know he didn't judge me because he had done much worse. It makes sense now. Our bonding over what I thought was a shared experience of miscarriage seems so shallow. I just don't see how I can get past this. What else has he not been truthful about?

Talking to God felt like one big complaint. Did this count as "sitting in silence" if her head was full of noise? She'd really never been formally taught how to pray, so she didn't know if she did it right. Why did it seem like everyone else had it figured out? No one else seemed to fidget in the pews or wrestle with what to say or how to pray. Sister Maria once told her prayer was all about an honest conversation with God, so did whining count? She also encouraged Violet not to assume that "everyone else" knew more, did more, and had "everything figured out."

It's really not fair. Not only did Tristan throw my life off course eight years ago, but now it's coming back to haunt me. I'm never going to escape it. I can never change what happened. Why couldn't I just stop drinking after one glass of wine? God, was this part of your bigger plan? Taking my babies' lives? How does that fit into the so-called loving narrative that you've written for the whole world? It was hard enough to go through that, to keep it a secret, and now, after all of this time, I finally find someone who loves me for me and accepts my flaws. Then it turns out that he really was too good to be true.

She sat back into the pew and shut her eyes, a small pool of tears stinging her lids. The oils of the incense became more overpowering. She crossed and uncrossed her legs a few times. Her head throbbed as she tried to hold back her tears. A couple salty drops found their way down her face and onto her lips. She slowly re-opened her eyes to see if anyone stared at her.

She fished around in her purse for anything to dab her tears away. She reached for her phone and decided against checking it, not wanting to spoil the peace of the moment. After a minute of turning over every knickknack in her purse, she settled back into the pew and resigned herself to using her shirtsleeve. Her forehead throbbed, and her jaw clenched. She didn't want to hold back her tears anymore. She emitted a small gasp and let the tears follow.

She couldn't remember the last time she'd really been in silence like this. Whether it was driving, running, or cleaning, she always had music or a podcast playing in the background.

After a few more minutes in the pew, she lingered in the vestibule and stopped at the bulletin board. There were flyers for a men's Saturday morning group, a mom's weekday Bible study with babysitting available, and a young adult group. If the youth group was anything like the crowd she'd been part of in Boston, there'd be a handful of arrogant men like Tristan, and some of them might even know him now. That made it a no-go.

There was also a table covered in pamphlets for overcoming addiction, healing from abuse, dealing with depression, etc. She wondered if the solution to all of this was to just move again to a place that definitely didn't involve any of her exes. But what would that solve? If she moved out of Maine, then it would prove that, once again, she was making life choices based on an ex-boyfriend. She didn't want to let them have that power.

She walked back to her car, but not ready to head home. She pulled out her phone and double-checked her texts. Nothing. She pulled up the HotelTonight app and found a last-minute deal on a cute, local bed-and-breakfast. It offered peace and quiet for $119. She couldn't put a price tag on a place to herself and the whole morning to sleep in.

When she checked in, she remembered that she had no luggage. However, her mom always taught her to be prepared, so the Merrimack College sweatpants and waffle T in her trunk would make for cozy sleepwear.

"Do you have a toothbrush and toothpaste?" Violet asked. "Oh, and possibly a razor?"

Without moving his eyes off the computer, the silver-haired man behind the counter in a navy suit opened up a drawer, pulled out the travel-size toiletries, and slid them toward her. She wondered if he ever got tired of distributing them to forgetful guests. "Thank you."

"Your room is on the third floor. If you walk down this hallway, you'll find the elevator and the stairs just a stone's throw farther."

When she reached her room, she threw her purse onto the desk and flopped onto the bed. Did today really happen? She was single now, and she was still the mother of two babies who she'd lost to miscarriage. How would she start over and ever meet someone? Maybe her punishment for all her poor choices was to be alone forever.

Chapter 21

———◆◆———

Violet woke to a sliver of sunshine cutting through an opening in the curtains. Her heart raced. What day was it? She fished around on her bed for her phone. What time was it? Noon? How had she slept this late? She had missed two calls from Sadie, plus five texts, including, "Where are you?" "Seriously, can you just answer?" and "Are you alive?"

There was nothing from Jude, but there was one text from Father Tristan. "Hey Vi," he wrote. "Can you give me a call when you get a chance?"

It didn't sound urgent, but she was intrigued. Did his use of "Vi" mean he thought they were on friendly terms after almost kissing? If so, she would set the record straight.

Had he heard about the end of her engagement somehow? Her stomach rolled. She picked up the room landline and dialed for the front desk. "Hi, is there any way I can get a late checkout?"

"Let me see, here." She heard the man typing. "How about one o'clock?"

"That would be great, thank you!"

It would be just enough time to take a long, luxurious shower and think about how to move forward in life. Her finger felt bare. She'd gotten used to playing with her ring, sliding it up and down her finger.

She stared at herself in the mirror before getting in the shower. A wisp of her blonde hair brushed her face, and she smiled gingerly. She moved closer to the mirror to see her freckles, which she had hated as a child. Her stomach wasn't flat. She had the proverbial love handles. Usually, she opted for self-deprecating comments about her body around friends. "I need to get rid of this spare tire around my midsection," she'd complain, earning the sympathy of her boozy brunch friends in Boston as they all sipped back mimosas and nodded in agreement.

Tristan had often been quick to remind her of how beautiful she was, and though she never wanted a guy to love her purely for her looks, it felt nice to hear a man found her attractive. Right now, though, she felt beautiful without anyone telling her. Perhaps, it was the first time. She couldn't help but think this was a victory: to feel beautiful without validation.

Sister Maria always reminded her that in God's eyes, everyone was beautiful because we're all made in his image and likeness, and he sees the beauty emanating from our hearts. Her words sounded great in theory, but in practice, they seemed unattainable. If God thought she was beautiful, what exactly did that do for Violet on Earth? Did it matter what God thought if she didn't believe in her own goodness? And if God thought everyone was beautiful, then how was she special?

After a long, warm shower, she was on the road back to Ogunquit with a wet, messy bun, and the same clothes from yesterday. She dialed Tristan through Bluetooth.

He picked up after two rings. "Violet, hi. Thanks for calling me back."

"No problem. What's up?" She feigned cheerfulness, trying not to reveal her heartbreak.

"I wanted to apologize about the other day. I crossed a line."

"That makes two of us. I appreciate your apology, and I'm glad you called because I've been thinking…" Violet sighed. "It would be best if we don't see each other anymore and don't have any sort of contact."

"I agree."

Violet exhaled with relief. "Thank you. I really do wish you the best. I'll keep you in my prayers."

"You'll be in mine, as well."

Violet paused, wondering if she should share her bad news. "I'm going to need those prayers. Look, I don't want to go into details, but Jude and I broke up. It had nothing to do with you or our past, but I'm going through a tough time right now." Was that true, though? It did have something to do with Tristan. Jude just didn't know.

"Whoa. I'm shocked. Are you ok?"

"Yes, I will be. Like I said, I don't want to continue down this path of opening ourselves up to each other emotionally, so let's just leave it at that."

"I respect that."

"Goodbye, Tristan," she said, and she hoped it was for the last time.

* * * * *

Violet wondered how she'd muster the energy to spend time with Harper. All she wanted was to lie in bed and order takeout, but she also hoped that Harper's zeal would raise her spirits. Sure enough, Harper greeted Violet with a big hug, a smile, and a twinkle in her eye.

"I colored you a picture." Harper handed Violet a white piece of paper with lots of colorful swirls.

"Harper, thank you so much. I love it! You must have had so much fun drawing this."

"I did it all by myself!"

"Wow. I'm so proud of you." Violet's heart ached at Harper's generosity. Would she ever have a family of her own with a daughter as sweet as Harper? If the twins were still here, she could see them getting along with Harper.

"Miss Violet, what happened to your ring?" Harper pointed to her bare finger.

Kids were so perceptive, but would a seven-year-old even understand a break-up? "I decided not to wear it today." It wasn't exactly a lie. It was more of a half-truth. The answer seemed to satisfy Harper because she didn't ask any more questions about it. Jude popped into Violet's head throughout the afternoon. Had they really broken up? Or was it a bad dream? Toward the end of the afternoon, one of the other volunteers, Mrs. Medina, came over.

"Oh, Violet! I heard the news about you and Jude. I'm so sorry!" Mrs. Medina reached out to hug her. How did Mrs. Medina know? Who was she kidding? Mrs. Medina knew everything about everybody. Violet didn't want to cry, but the tears came freely.

"Miss Violet, why are you crying? Are you sad?" Harper asked.

"Yes," Violet muffled. She used her pointer fingers to blot out her tears.

"I'm sorry. I didn't mean to make you cry. If it's any consolation, I had two failed engagements before I met my husband."

It wasn't consolation, but Violet appreciated Mrs. Medina's good intentions.

"Why are you sad?" Harper asked.

How did one explain this to a child? "Remember when I told you I was going to get married?" Violet squatted to meet Harper's eyes.

"Your fancy?"

Violet broke into a small smile. "Yes, my fiancé. He and I broke up."

"You broke up? What does that mean?" Harper asked.

"It means that we're not going to get married anymore."

"Why?"

Why did kids have to be so curious sometimes? "Adult reasons. You'll understand when you grow up."

Harper hugged Violet's legs.

"Don't worry," Mrs. Medina continued. "There will be someone else." *Ah, yes, the age-old "wisdom" after a break-up.*

Violet thanked her, but she really wanted to reply, "Easy for you to say." She reminded herself that Mrs. Medina was just trying to be nice and supportive, but she made a mental note to never tell another woman that "there will be someone else" because really there was no guarantee. And no one could compare to Jude.

Chapter 22

ONE MONTH LATER

———•———

"Where are we going?" Violet groaned. They were about twenty minutes into a drive that Sadie sprung on her that morning.

"You'll see when we get there."

Violet reclined the passenger seat and shut her eyes. "I'll nap then."

"Suit yourself. It'll take about three more hours. Because you won't be awake to keep me company, I'll play some music to pass the time."

Violet waved her hand. "Ugh."

"You're no fun!"

"Sorry I missed the memo stating that people who just broke up with their fiancé are supposed to be happy and energetic."

"It's been a month, Vi, and you're right. There is no such memo, but there also isn't one that says you're entitled to be a brat."

"Sadie, you practically plucked me from my bed this morning. You gave me two minutes to get into the car," Violet said. "And I have my period." She rummaged around for a towel or a shirt to spread across her eyes so she could sleep.

"Alright, Sleeping Beauty, as you wish. We shall drive in silence until we reach the palace."

* * * * *

Sadie's cold hands stirred Violet awake. She squinted to adjust to the light. Hills of vibrant grass surrounded them and stretched for miles. Perhaps this is what inspired Julie Andrews to sing "the hills are alive" in *The Sound of Music*.

"Woah…"

"We're here."

"Which is where?" Violet asked.

"Divine Mercy Shrine."

Violet jolted. "In Stockbridge?"

"Yes."

"I've always wanted to come here. How did you know?"

"You mentioned it a couple of times, and let's be real. You're one of those uber Catholics who loves anything with the name shrine," Sadie replied. "C'mon, let's go." She hopped out of the car. Violet grabbed her sunglasses and put them on.

"I have a whole day planned for us."

"Who are you?" Violet laughed. "I thought you would make me go hiking or something."

"Well, I only pulled this together last night. It was just a couple of Google searches, so don't set your expectations too high."

Violet looped her arm around Sadie's and started walking toward the shrine. "I'm just glad to be with my much older and wiser sister for the day," Violet winked.

"Much wiser, yes. Much older, no."

Trees lined the street on their walk from the parking lot to the main part of Eden Hill, the marquee sight: the National Shrine of Divine Mercy. Only a few other people were there. It was a Thursday afternoon, after all. They strolled mostly in silence, inhaling the fresh flowers. They basked in the serenity of hundreds of acres of nature.

"This reminds me of the countryside in Ireland," Sadie said.

"You've never been to Ireland."

"I know, but if I went, I imagine that this is exactly what it would look like. It's really peaceful."

They stopped outside the massive stone church and slowly ascended the stairs to the shrine. An older, hunched-over man was leaving and held the large, wooden door open for them. "Thank you." Violet picked up her pace so the frail man wouldn't have to hold it for long.

"Enjoy." He smiled.

Violet and Sadie walked inside, turning to look at each other and exchange glances of wonder and awe. They didn't say a word. As much as Sadie hated religion, Violet knew her sister loved beautiful places, including churches. They each lingered at the stained glass windows and the mosaics inside, creating a kaleidoscope of color.

They enjoyed the rest of the afternoon in their tranquil cadence, rarely stopping to speak to each other but understanding each other still the same. Though Sadie didn't like attending church, Violet thought she was respectful during Mass Looking over at Sadie after receiving Communion, Violet said extra prayers of thanksgiving for her sister.

They stayed after Mass to recite the Divine Mercy Chaplet. To be honest, Violet much preferred praying the Chaplet over the Rosary. She giggled as Sadie struggled through, unable to remember what to say and clearly wondering when it would all end. When they used to accompany their mom to the weekly Divine Mercy Chaplet at church, they'd each bring their own bright Rosary beads and pretend to know the prayers, silently mouthing random words.

"Before we get lunch, I want to show you something," Sadie said as they walked out of the church.

"Ooh! Another surprise."

They sauntered across the grassy plain behind the church. Sadie pointed to a building a bit farther off. "That's where we're going."

Violet stopped for a beat. "Can we just lie on the grass for a bit?"

"Why not?"

Violet plopped onto the grass on her back, facing a large, white, outdoor shrine, a stark contrast to the verdant grass.

"So what we're looking at now is the Mother of Mercy Outdoor Shrine, according to the map, at least," Sadie said.

Violet shook her head in amazement. "It's so overpowering and beautiful. I wonder if they ever celebrate Mass outside here." She let out months, and maybe years, of pent-up sadness in a shrill cry.

"Feel better?"

"Yes." Violet stood, wiping the grass stains off her pants. "I'm ready now."

As they approached the entrance of their next destination, she noticed two giant angels flanking a blue door. Their wings formed an archway to the Shrine of the Holy Innocents. Little baby footprints etched into the ground led them inside, where soft, lilting music greeted them.

"This is a shrine for unborn children and other children who died," Sadie explained.

Violet clutched her chest. She rooted herself in a moment of stillness, overcome with the scent of lavender. "What? I didn't know this was here." Her throat went dry. The inside of the shrine teemed with different shades of yellow, green, blue, and purple glass tiles lining all of the walls. Violet gravitated toward the kneelers in front of the statue of Our Lady of Guadalupe. She knelt down and made the sign of the cross.

In the name of the Father, and of the Son, and of the Holy Spirit. Amen. Lord, thank you for bringing me here today, especially since I'm here with Sadie. I don't know what's going on in my life, but I know you know all things, so if you could just enlighten me, I'd really appreciate it. Please, please give me a sign that you are with my babies and you're taking care of them. I pray we have a safe drive back to Maine. Our Lady of Guadalupe, pray for us. Amen.

Violet rose from the kneeler and ran her hands over the cool, colorful tiles engraved with the names of the lost children. The tiles gave her comfort that other people knew her heartbreak intimately. How were the parents of these children feeling now? Did they think about their children every day like she did? She wondered about the story behind each child's death. Had any been like hers? She hoped they were all playing together in Heaven with her twins.

"I can't believe this," Violet whispered.

Sadie nodded and rubbed her back. "It's ok."

Violet sniffled and started to whimper. "I never got to hold them."

"I know, I know." Sadie stroked Violet's hair. "I want to show you something."

Sadie led Violet farther down the room past a fountain to another section of the colorful wall. "Take a look." Sadie pointed to a mint-colored tile.

Lily & John Paul, beloved twins of Violet and Tristan.

Violet gasped. "Did you…"

Sadie nodded. "Mom helped."

Violet choked on her sobs. The tile was the only tangible sign of the twins. "I just…don't have words," Violet uttered. "I thought you said you cooked up this idea last night."

Sadie smirked. "I lied a little. But it was worth it."

"How long has our tile been here?"

"I got a call that it was installed last week, and I tried to figure out a way to surprise you. Then, with everything that happened with Jude, I wasn't sure if the timing was right. Anyway, last night, it dawned on me to just do the damn thing!"

"I can never thank you enough." She kissed Sadie on the cheek.

"Are you ok with it saying Tristan's name on there, too? Mom and I went back and forth on what to write."

Violet tucked a piece of tear-soaked hair behind her ear. "Yes, of course. It's true. They were his babies, too. Just writing 'Violet's twins' wouldn't have been the whole truth."

"We figured it was safer to not put the last name because people know him as Father Tristan now."

"Smart. I wish Mom was here to see it, too."

"I know, but she's working. I felt like it was important for us to do this today and get you out of your funk."

"I'm not sure we accomplished that," Violet said. "I feel like a hot mess."

"And you look like it, too," Sadie laughed.

Violet flopped her head on Sadie's shoulder. "You're the best."

"Alright, I've completely exhausted my limit for serious stuff for a good month, so let's get something to eat. I found a place a few minutes away."

"Sounds good to me. By the way, do you think I should tell Tristan about this?" Violet asked. "I mean, we don't talk anymore. I told him I didn't want any contact…"

"I don't know. It's up to you. It seems like every time you two talk, something dramatic happens."

"You're right. I'll just keep it to myself." They walked in silence for a bit, their arms looped, making their way back up the grassy hill. "You know, I think this would be good for Jude, too," Violet said. "I think it would give him some peace."

"Have you talked to him at all?"

Violet shook her head.

"Has he tried to reach out to you?"

"Nope." Violet felt her lips quiver.

"You miss him, don't you?"

Violet nodded. Sadie pulled her in closer and rested her head against her shoulder. "I'm sure he misses you, too."

"I hope so, too."

A few days ago, she'd seen his face on one of the real estate signs outside of a house for sale. Why had she been so hard on him about keeping the abortion secret? He was scared, just like she had been. In the moment, it felt good to make him feel like it was his fault for their break-up, but that comfort faded quickly. She'd been a coward to let him think it was all his fault and not tell him about how she'd gone behind his back to see Tristan and almost kissed him.

Chapter 23

THREE MONTHS LATER

———•●•———

Violet jingled her car keys as she leaned against the trunk of her car and checked her Fitbit watch. Tristan was five minutes late. She inhaled the salty, ocean air. Yesterday, he had texted her, asking to meet her to share some "good news." This was in direct violation of their agreement to not contact each other, but he'd assured her that this was an urgent exception. She'd said ok on the condition that it be in public at a busy parking lot. Granted that was where they fell into temptation the first time, but now she was on guard.

She thought a long time about what to wear, perhaps too long for such a casual encounter. She didn't want to make it look like she'd dressed up for Tristan, but at the same time, she still wanted to look nice. She'd settled on a pair of pink, woven cotton pants and a flowy, white T-shirt with a light blue crystal dangle necklace.

What could Tristan possibly want to talk about? What was good news for a priest? Maybe his dad was engaged? There's no way that would qualify as urgent. Her thoughts were interrupted when she saw his car pull into the lot. He wasn't wearing his white collar as he normally would, but then again, she didn't know the rules for priests. She waved. He parked a couple of spots over from her and stepped out.

"Thanks so much for meeting me," he said as he approached her.

"Sure," she replied. "It sounded important."

He smiled. "I think I need to give you a little bit of context. These past few months have been completely life-changing for me. I've spent a lot of time in prayer and discernment. Violet, I'm leaving the priesthood."

She cocked her head and held up her hands. "What?"

Tristan nodded. "It's something that's been on my mind, even before I met you, but when you came back into my life, it put everything into focus."

"But you were ordained just over a year and a half ago."

Tristan shook his head. "I know, but I wasn't honest in my discernment process. I shouldn't have gotten ordained."

"Then why did you?"

"I didn't want to disappoint anyone."

There has to be more to this story because he never seemed to mind disappointing me. She wanted to roll her eyes and grunt, but she held herself back. She folded her arms across her chest. "That's it? You finally decided that you didn't care about disappointing anyone anymore?"

"Well, I think leaving the priesthood would've happened eventually. You expedited the process, in a sense."

"Me?" *How is this my fault?*

"Well, not directly. When you reappeared in my life, it made me think about things I buried long ago. They needed to come to the surface."

"I didn't know priests could just leave."

"Technically, I will always be a priest, but I've been given permission to step away from the clerical duties of celebrating Mass, hearing confessions, and administering sacraments."

Violet took a deep breath. "Wow." *But why is he telling me all of this?*

"A few months ago, I talked to the Bishop about what I've been going through and the regrets I have about my decisions," Tristan elaborated. "I asked him for permission to discern my future away from the priesthood. I went on a thirty-day Ignatian spiritual retreat, and during that time, I felt peace that the priesthood is not for me, and perhaps I was never called to it to begin with."

"Your Bishop must've been disappointed."

"He was, but he understood."

"There's such a shortage of priests, too."

"I know." Tristan sulked. "I feel bad about that."

"So what are you going to do? Are you going back to work in finance?"

"Not right away, but yes, I will go back to being a regular person with a job. I won't have any financial support from the Church anymore."

Violet nodded. "I think that's fair."

"I didn't want to tell anyone about it until it was a for-sure thing, and just this week, I received word that the Pope is letting me go from my vow of celibacy."

Violet raised her eyebrows. *That concerns me how?*

"It would allow me to get married in the Catholic Church and have a family."

Violet's heart started racing. Was he trying to make a move? "That's great. I'm happy for you."

"This is why I wanted to tell you in person." He paused and looked off for a beat. "I'd like to date you, for real this time, if you'll let me."

What is happening? "Tristan, I'm sorry if you felt like I was leading you on, and I admit that my attraction may have gotten the better of me a few months ago, but if you did this for me..."

"I made this decision without any guarantee that you'd even give me a chance." He reached for her cheek, but she gently pushed his hand away. "Violet, I feel like we never really had our chance."

"But we did," she protested.

"It's different now. I've changed. You've changed. I can't live with myself if I don't discern what a future with you would be like."

Violet's eyes bubbled with tears. She wiped the first droplets away. "Tristan, this is a lot. I don't...I don't know whether this is what I want."

"I thought you and Jude weren't together anymore?"

Violet scowled. Who did Tristan think he was? "We're not, but that doesn't mean I go running back to you."

He reached for her hands, but she pulled back. "I'd like us to try. I want to be with you."

"I'm...shocked." She took a deep breath, inhaling for three seconds and exhaling for seven seconds as she gripped the skin between her eyes. "I'm not leaving the Church. I love being Catholic."

"I'm not leaving either," Tristan said. "I'll just be sitting in the pews instead of serving on the altar." His eyes pleaded for love. He used his finger to gently trace the outline of her hand. It sent a jolt of electricity to her skin, and she didn't resist. "It feels like a lot of pressure, to be totally honest. I mean, it was just a few months ago that my engagement ended. My heart hasn't fully healed. You're asking me to be serious about this with you, and then what?"

"I'm hoping marriage..."

Marriage? She shivered. When they dated eight years ago, it was for ten months, and any hint of engagement or any type of commitment, for that matter, was tamped down like a small fire. *"Let's just be happy now,"* he'd always say, kissing her on the forehead three times. It was always about the present to him. Now, after all of these years, he was talking about the future and permanent commitment.

Suddenly, Jude's face flashed before her: his twinkling chocolate eyes and the burgeoning crow's feet around them that he refused to acknowledge. She thought of the commitment he wanted to make to her and her unwillingness to follow through. She never had to convince Jude to be with her.

Now, a man who she'd previously begged for a commitment was standing right in front of her. Tristan reached to stroke her hair, and she surprised herself by letting him. "I will never forgive myself if I don't seize this opportunity. Ever since I heard your voice in the confessional, I've wondered why. 'Why God? Why would you bring her back into my life?'"

"But Tristan, I don't want to go back," Violet said. "There were so many bad memories there. Time has a way of putting a rose-colored lens over some things, but it's a protective mechanism. I know better than to fantasize about our past relationship."

"That's just it. I don't fantasize about it. I just think of the potential. Violet, we're both grown up now. You met me at one of the lowest points in my life."

Violet inhaled. "I suppose." She squinted under the summer sun.

"You don't need to make any decisions right now, but would you please read this letter?" He took a folded piece of notebook paper and handed it to her. "It contains all my thoughts on paper and will sound a lot more coherent than what I've said today."

"Ok," she hesitated.

"Thank you. After you read it, please let me know if you want to see me. If I don't hear from you, I'll take that as your response and leave you alone." Tristan opened his arms for a hug, which Violet accepted. What had she just signed up for? She was eager to open the letter, but she drove straight home instead, contemplating what it might contain before finally opening it in her driveway.

Dear Violet,

As you know, I've never enjoyed writing. It's a wonder I made it through grad school, but here are some thoughts I've cobbled together after multiple drafts.

I've never been at peace with how things ended between us. It felt like there was an ellipsis to our story...not a period. Not an ending.

Somehow we've found our way back into each other's lives. I marvel at how this happened, neither through my intention or yours.

At first, I questioned it, but now I only feel gratitude. It feels like a second chance for us, but more so for me. It's a second chance for me to regard you as the beautiful woman that you are.

I never said these words when we dated before, but I love you.

I'm quite aware that my actions did not show that I loved you. Yes, I was strongly attracted, and yes, I enjoyed your company more than anyone else's, but the real hard work of loving you was something I never did.

I never showed you how much I admired and cherished you and how utterly inadequate I felt to be loved by you.

When you told me that you loved me, and I didn't say it back, I hated myself. I didn't want to make that commitment because I knew I'd fall short of loving anyone.

It felt wiser at the time to pretend I didn't love you.

When you finally had enough of me and said goodbye, I was numb. My greatest fear of you leaving me had come true, and it was my fault. It wasn't me you really rejected. You rejected a shell of me: a man, or rather a boy, who was bruised, proud, and scared.

I hope you can finally see the real me today. To be loved by you would be the greatest honor, but I know our future is not mine alone to decide.

No matter what happens, I will always love and care for you.

Tris

Chapter 24

———•———

Without consulting anyone, Violet agreed to meet with Tristan again. He was intent on calling it a date, unlike eight years ago, when they always "just hung out." She hated thinking of their relationship back then as more of a friends-with-benefits situation, but Sadie was right to call it that.

She pulled into the parking lot of a state park. They chose a place about an hour north of Portland so that they were less likely to run into anyone they knew. Tristan was already there, sitting on a bench, dressed in jeans and a gray, long-sleeve waffle shirt that hugged his biceps. Age had been kind to him, she had to admit. Could it be that he was even more handsome with a few more years of wisdom and a twinge of silver on his sideburns? *Don't be deceived by his good looks, though.*

She briefly considered running toward him so he could scoop her up and swing her around, like Jude had done when she accepted his proposal. Instead, she proceeded slowly.

How would she greet him? A hug? A handshake was too formal. Maybe just a wave? "This is so weird." Her face heated. *Be open, be open.*

"Definitely not conventional." He stood up, showed her a big wicker basket filled with lunch, and then leaned forward for a side hug.

"What did you bring?"

He opened the lid to show a baguette, some cheese, grapes, and berries. "I remember how much you like roast beef on a pretzel bun with potato chips, so I have that here as well."

Wow, he remembers. "I'm impressed," Violet beamed.

"I figured we could eat over there," he pointed ahead.

"There's some nice shade if you want, or we can sit in one of the sunny patches."

Violet pondered the options. "Let's sit in the sun." She took a seat on the flannel blanket Tristan splayed on the grass and started massaging her temples. Why did she feel so nervous?

"Is something wrong?" he asked.

"No, I'm laughing at how life works out. A year ago, I would never have seen this coming."

"Isn't there that saying, 'If you want to make God laugh, tell Him your plans.'"

She rolled her eyes. "That's so trite. That makes it seem like whatever we want is different from what God wants. That's not always true. God puts desires in our hearts."

"What are your desires?"

"Right now, it would be a warm roast beef sandwich." She purposely wove the conversation away from serious talk.

Violet took a bite of the warm sandwich, the Swiss cheese melting in her mouth. She relished the combination of the salted bun and the cheese, a savory juxtaposition. It was a welcome break from conversation, to chew and swallow, with no expectations of talking.

Tristan poured sparkling grape juice into a plastic champagne glass and passed it to her.

"Fancy," she said. "Do you not drink anymore?"

"I do, occasionally, but not like when we dated."

Thank God. Violet nodded. When they had dated, she constantly wondered whether what she said would push him away or make him question their relationship, like the time she brought up being exclusive. It seemed a reasonable request after four months of dating, but he'd gotten mad and told her not to mention it again.

Now, the roles were reversed. He was gunning for her attention and affection. If she wanted to be with him, he would be hers. She could ask him questions without fear of him leaving. She was ensconced, but why didn't the thought of playing "hard to get" excite her? Perhaps her "justice gene," as her mom called it, weakened and was now reserved for more serious matters than petty revenge on an ex. In some ways, though, she felt like the same young woman who'd fallen in love with Tristan O'Connor.

After they finished eating, she scooted next to him and rested her head on his shoulder. He wrapped his arm around her and kissed the top of her head. It felt natural. If things had been different, she thought, they might be here right now with their twins. It would be a family picnic, not just a first date for two ex-lovers.

"Do you ever think about them? What they would've been like?" she asked, not needing to explicitly say "the twins."

"Every day."

In the distance, Violet saw an empty playground where the swings stirred in the soft breeze. "They would be heading into second grade soon."

"That's crazy."

She wiped her eyes. "I need to stop myself before I get too sentimental. I don't want to wonder forever."

"It's ok."

She lifted her head and faced him. She slowly traced the outline of his jaw with her pointer finger. His eyes were shiny with tears, too. She took the plunge and buried her face in his neck. Tristan cradled her, letting his own tears fall onto her head. Blonde tendrils of her hair clung to her face, matted down by the dampness.

"Have you ever wondered? Was it two girls? Two boys? One of each?" Tristan asked.

She sat up and looked into Tristan's eyes. "Oh, I guess I never told you. When I miscarried, the doctor confirmed that it was a boy and a girl."

"It's strange, but I had a feeling it was a boy and a girl. Did you pick names?"

"Lily and John Paul."

"I like those," Tristan said. "John Paul was my Confirmation name."

"Really?"

"Yep. I really like Saint Pope John Paul II."

"I never knew that."

"I guess we never really talked about that stuff when we were dating."

Violet sighed. "There's a lot we didn't talk about."

He took a slow breath. "I'm sorry. I want to do this the right way with you now."

"The funny thing is that eight years ago, I would have given anything to hear you say exactly that." She pulled at a couple blades of grass.

"Would you have really wanted to be with me, after how I treated you?"

"Back then? Of course. Tristan, I could see that you weren't *you* most of the time we were together. There were glimpses where I saw this kind, gentle giant of a man. I knew you were fighting something inside, that you were broken, and you just couldn't love me then. But..." She looked out over the grassy plain, unruly in some areas and clearly in need of some landscaping. "I thought I could be the woman who you'd love enough and care enough about to inspire you to change." She shook her head, laughing. "It's so silly to think about now because of course you can't change people, but back then, I thought that if I stuck around long enough, I could heal you or something."

"I never felt worthy of you."

She furrowed her brow. "You certainly didn't act that way. You treated me like dirt a lot."

"I was pushing you away. I didn't want you to see the real me. I didn't want to get hurt."

"A lot of good that did. We both got hurt." She kept her eyes on Tristan as a tiny tear trickled down her face. He reached for her clasped hands, kissed them slowly, and then nestled his nose against them.

She heaved a sigh. "You know, I blame myself for the twins not being here."

"Why?"

"It really is my fault, and I'm not looking for your reassurance otherwise."

Tristan nodded.

She bit her lip. How would she get through this story without crying? "About two months after we broke up, I really missed you. I didn't want to call or text you because I knew I'd just be thrown back into that toxic web. I had just found out I was having twins, and I felt overwhelmed. I thought you should know about the babies, and I had every intention to tell you."

"I understand why you didn't," Tristan said.

"I almost did, though. I went to Molly's Pub one night, mostly hoping I'd run into you. I thought maybe if I 'accidentally' saw you there, we would talk, and I'd find the courage to tell you about the pregnancy." Violet closed her eyes and put herself back inside the local dive. "You were there."

"I was? I don't remember seeing you after we dated."

She shook her head. "You didn't. You were sitting at the bar, making out with some girl. My heart sank. There I was, carrying your babies, and it looked like you had just so easily moved on. That's when I knew that I really had to do it all alone."

Tristan was stoic but opened his mouth to reply.

She held up her hand. "Please, just let me finish." She cleared her throat. "I just wasn't in my right mind. I had no idea what I was going to do. Here I was, this good Catholic girl, and I couldn't bear the thought of everyone finding out I was pregnant and unwed. Especially on TV. It felt so public. I played out the scene in my head where the station did a send-off segment for me, wishing me luck with the babies, with no mention of a father or a husband. It was absolutely humiliating. I didn't want to disappoint my mom after all she'd done to raise Sadie and me the right way and not repeat her life as a single mom. But there I was, making the same mistake. So, that night after seeing you with that girl, I went home and got completely wasted. I was blackout drunk. The next morning, I woke up on the floor of my bathroom in the most excruciating pain with a pool of blood down there. I sensed I'd lost the babies, and it was a scarier thought than anything I'd ever experienced. Sadie drove me to the hospital immediately. I lost the babies. It's my fault." Her head throbbed as she tried to stifle her tears. "Why did that have to happen? Why couldn't I have just coped with my emotions in a healthier way? Those poor babies never had a chance to live because of me."

"Violet, no, no. Of course not. It's not your fault." He reached for her.

She slapped his wrist away. "Don't say that. You know it's my fault. It doesn't help to deny it. I need to live with this. I have been living with this." She fell back onto the grass and wiped away her tears. "Two lives were entrusted to me, and I let them down."

"No, you didn't. I'm the one who let all of you down," Tristan laid down next to her and looked into her eyes. "If I could go back, I would in a heartbeat. I would have proposed to you, married you, and taken care of you."

"But you didn't. It doesn't matter what you would have done."

"I know. I know you're right. Is there anything I can do to show you how truly sorry I am for being a jerk and not treating you right?"

Violet shook her head. "No. I forgive you plain and simple. I don't want to hold anything over you. It doesn't do anyone any good."

"They're our little intercessors up in Heaven. They're happier than we'll ever be or could ever fathom here on Earth."

She nodded in agreement and looked him in the eye, seeing her own reflection. Why was it so much easier to forgive him than herself?

Chapter 25

To Tristan's delight, Violet accepted a second date, and he wanted this one to be fun: no reminiscing about the past or what could have been.

He waited in his car outside a laser tag place, anticipating Violet's arrival. She was cute in her mid-twenties, but now she was truly beautiful, a little fuller all around. He thought she was almost too skinny when they had dated before.

She tapped on his window, interrupting his thoughts. Could he just sweep her away and make love to her right now? He didn't want to go there mentally, out of respect for her, but it was hard not to think about it with her right in front of him.

"You ready?" He stepped out of the car.

"Yea! Don't I look dressed for the occasion?"

Yes, but I'd like you undressed. She had on loose, black joggers and a zip-up hoodie from her alma mater. As they approached the entrance, he reached for her hand. She squeezed back with reassurance.

Violet had no mercy for him as they played on opposite teams. She rubbed it in that her team beat his team in the first go-around, but he came back to obliterate her team the second time. The teasing made their banter easy, and they were both sweating by the end. He wished he could just pull her close for a kiss.

"Where do you want to go for dinner?" he asked as they walked back to their cars.

"I'd love some pizza."

"I'll never say no to pizza," Tristan said. "Why don't we take my car? I can drive you back to yours after?"

She hesitated a moment.

"Or whatever you want," he said.

"We can take your car." She slid into the passenger side.

He put the key into the ignition. Was now the right time for a kiss? He turned toward her. "I don't know any places around here, so let me just look online to find a good spot."

"I know a place," she said. "I'll lead you. Just drive."

Tristan followed Violet's direction, his hands clenched around the steering wheel, growing sweaty. He wanted to kiss her. It was like high school all over again. Would sitting in his car outside a pizza shop really work? Or should he wait until after? The anticipation of finally getting to kiss her after waiting over seven years excited him. Small talk consumed the rest of their drive until they pulled up outside a place called Pizza Heaven.

"Nice," Tristan said. "Sounds perfect to me."

Violet hopped out of the car as soon as he parked. No kiss just yet.

* * * * *

When they got back into the car after dinner, Violet buckled up and reached for the radio as he turned the car on.

"Violet." He sat still and waited for her to look at him.

"What's up?" she asked, tuning through the radio stations.

"I love you."

She froze and turned toward him. Had he said too much too soon? His heart raced.

"I think I love you, too," she said.

Tristan felt the shackles on his heart break off. He held her gaze and gently stroked the side of her face. Unlike in the parking lot a few months prior, she didn't pull away when he leaned in to kiss her. How he had missed her lips.

Chapter 26

———●———

Sister Maria's light blue eyes twinkled, and the sun reflected off the mosaic of wrinkles on her face as she listened to Violet talk about her reunion with Tristan, including their kiss from a few nights ago. She had stopped by Violet's place on her way to northern Maine for a retreat.

"I think I love him. I told him so."

Sister Maria grinned. "I thought you might say that."

"Really?"

"Why, yes. Everything you've told me up to this point indicates your strong feelings for him, and I already knew you cared about him."

"I don't know what to do, though. He has all but asked me to marry him, and I don't know if I would accept a proposal."

"May I tell you a story?"

"Please," Violet said, relieved not to dwell on her own saga for a bit.

Sister Maria looked past Violet, fixated on a memory, it seemed. Her eyes fluttered open and closed a few times as she wrapped her wrinkly hands around the blue mug in front of her. "As I've told you many times, I entered the convent when I was twenty-five, but that was actually the second time. The first time, I was twenty-two."

"I never knew that."

"Yes. I met a man while I was in my first year. I was just a postulant." Sister Maria looked off in the way a lover does to reminisce on a beautiful day gone past. Violet never thought of Sister Maria being in love with anyone other than Jesus.

"It was purely by accident that I met him. I was working at the local Catholic school, and he was a teacher there. He was a few years older, and we didn't mean to fall in love, but we did."

"That must've been so confusing." *Maybe Sister Maria does understand my plight.*

"Oh, it was. I prayed to the Good Lord every day, asking for His will. We never kissed or went on a date, but I grew so fond of him because we saw each other every day at the school. We talked in between classes and found ourselves volunteering at the same events to be near each other more."

"Did he ask you to leave the convent?" She pictured Sister Maria flirting with the mystery man.

"No, never! He was such a gentleman, a true man of God. He respected my state in life. He never asked me out or gave me gifts. I don't want you to get the wrong idea. It was obvious to us, and to others, that we were in love, but we didn't act on it. My Mother Superior suggested I really discern where God was leading me. She wasn't worried with numbers at the convent. She only wanted women to stay who truly felt called to a religious life. So, at that time, I discerned to leave and explore a relationship with this man."

"Oh! Wait, what was his name? I don't think you mentioned…"

"Richard." She smiled. She took a sip of her tea, basking in a memory. "I told him my decision, and he courted me. It was beautiful. He was the kindest man I'd ever known. My family loved him."

"So what went wrong?" Violet feared Sister Maria was about to describe a gruesome death that tore the two lovers apart.

"In the same way that I discerned to leave the convent, we discerned marriage. I decided to go back."

"To the convent?"

Sister Maria nodded.

"I don't understand. It sounds like everything was going well." Violet reached for one of the tea cookies on the center plate.

"I didn't feel much peace when I pictured my life as a wife and mother. It didn't feel like my calling. I thought of the convent and felt a wave of…tranquility and joy. It was clear in my heart that God was leading me there."

"But you had already been there and decided to leave."

"Yes, and I did that freely. I loved Richard freely, and I chose to return to religious life freely. Only when you can say no can you really say yes. I could say yes to God because I wholeheartedly said no to other options. If I had never left the convent, I may have always wondered what a life with Richard would be like. I was blessed to have that experience."

"But did something bad happen between you and him?"

Sister Maria gave a light wave of her hand in dismissal. "Oh no, dear. It wasn't personal. He would have been an excellent husband and father. It was Richard's love and safety that led me to where I am. He gave me the courage to say yes. It was clear to him toward the end of our relationship that I wanted to go back, and I was ready. I never regret what happened."

Violet frowned. "My heart hurts for Richard."

"He was heartbroken, yes, but he got over it. He actually drove me back to the convent when I re-entered. He said he could tell I was called to this life and that it must mean he was called to a different life, as well. As much as it hurt him, he knew the Lord had plans for him that he couldn't see."

Sister Maria took a sip of tea, her pinky finger pointed in the air.

"Well, you both have faith that I don't have."

"It's there for you, too. Ask the Lord to fill you with it. It's a free gift."

Violet shrugged. "If you say so."

Sister Maria zeroed her gaze on Violet. "Now, my dear. I didn't tell you this story to get all somber about love. My choice brought me joy. There was heartache, too, because I loved Richard, but I never felt like God made me join. It was an act of free will. I wanted it. Just because someone is called to religious life doesn't mean that they lose the capacity to fall in love with other people."

Violet thought of Tristan.

"My point is, we are called to love uniquely," Sister Maria continued. "For me, it wasn't a matter of Jesus versus Richard. Maybe that is what it seemed like to the greater world. No matter what I chose, I loved Jesus first, but I asked the Lord: How do you want me to grow in love? What is my school of love to be?"

"I know mine is marriage. I just don't know with whom." Violet shook her head.

"Is this because a part of you still thinks about Jude?" Sister Maria asked.

Violet nodded and sniffed to stifle her tears. "I shouldn't think of him. I was the one who ended the engagement."

"I can tell your heart is torn. Our hearts can care for more than one person, but we can only choose one to commit our lives to."

Violet opened her mouth to protest Sister Maria's observation but stopped herself. What was the point? She couldn't hide the truth from her mentor.

"Tristan loves me, but if I choose to be with him, I know it won't bring the twins back. On the other hand, it's silly to think that Jude is even an option for me anymore. He could be dating another woman for all I know. I really hurt him, and I wouldn't blame him for never wanting to talk to me again. But when I think of home I think of Jude."

"Violet, marriage is a long road, regardless of the man you marry. What is God telling you? How is he moving your heart?"

Violet shook her head. "I don't know. Why is this so confusing? It's like life is a puzzle, and God is up there laughing at my attempts to figure it out."

Sister Maria laughed. "Oh, Violet. You have always been the thinker. Perhaps we don't need to talk about it. Maybe you just need to leave it at Jesus' feet and ask him to carry this burden that is clearly so heavy on your heart."

"I suppose." Violet bit her lip and fixed her gaze on the dusty floor. It was Sadie's week to clean the bungalow. She'd have to remind her again, as usual. "You know, I never asked you, but why didn't you tell me that Tristan already knew about the twins because of your note?"

Sister Maria bobbed her head a few times. "I thought you might find out eventually."

"I recognized your handwriting, but Tristan had no idea it was you."

She frowned. "I am sorry. Truly. Perhaps it was not my place. I'm not a saint, after all. I thought he should know, and after you lost the twins, you were adamant about not talking to him. If you decided to tell him someday, I wanted you to do so from your own desire, not to appease me or anyone else. In the meantime, I thought he should know so that he could pray for the twins and ask for their intercession."

Violet flinched. "I'm not mad at you. I was just surprised that he had known all this time and never said anything."

"So did you."

"True," she sighed, not realizing her own hypocrisy until now. "So what ever happened to Richard? What did he end up doing?"

"You know him."

"I do?" Violet crinkled her nose, wracking her brain for men of Sister Maria's age.

Sister Maria smiled, and her eyes lit up. "Father Rick Goren."

Chapter 27

If Tristan had to point to one trait that annoyed him most about his dad, it was that Skip O'Connor was messy. Cluttered was perhaps a better word. He wasn't one to have four-day-old, crusted lasagna clinging to a dinner plate. He was more of a papers-here-there-and-everywhere kind of guy. There was no rhyme or reason to his organization. If Tristan couldn't find something in his dad's home, like an old album or a trinket from his childhood, then his dad would likely be of no help either. He would assure Tristan that it had never been thrown out, and thus it had to be *somewhere*, which was never reassuring. Most likely, his dad's shortcomings in this arena had led to Tristan's militant cleanliness and order. Tristan couldn't stand the disarray, but he was willing to endure it this afternoon for what he expected to be an important talk. He let himself in, dodging the various items on the floor to make his way to the kitchen.

"Why aren't you wearing your collar? Ain't that required of you?" His dad licked the white donut hole powder from his fingers. He passed Tristan some coffee.

"Normally, yes. Actually, that's why I came to talk to you today." Tristan repurposed a yellowed envelope as a coaster for his mug. He sighed. Where to start? "What would you say if I told you I'm leaving the priesthood so that I can get married and have a family someday?"

His dad laughed, but Tristan's expression didn't change.

"Dad, I'm serious."

He cleared his throat. "So you're thinking of abandoning your parishioners? There's already a shortage of priests."

Tristan knew it wouldn't be easy to convince his father. "This isn't a decision I made lightly. Please try to see it from my perspective."

"Alright, go on," his dad waved for him to continue.

"Do you remember that girl Violet I dated years back?" Tristan asked.

His dad smiled. "Ahh, I see where this is going."

Tristan launched into their unlikely reunion and his subsequent decision to take some time off to discern.

His dad stood from his seat and rubbed his hand down his face. "Give me one minute." He heard his dad moving a few boxes around in another room. *Great.* Whatever he was looking for, it would take way more than one minute to find. Tristan settled into his chair and looked around. He didn't know how Elaine, his dad's new girlfriend, put up with the clutter. Granted, they didn't live together, but if his dad ever remarried, he couldn't imagine Elaine wanting to live in disarray. The mess had annoyed his mother, but he knew that even if the house had been spick-and-span, she still would have clutched the bottle. In fact, his dad hadn't been too messy before she left. Rather, more of the hoarding, if he'd dare let you call it that, came after she'd left him for good.

"Ah! Here it is!" his dad yelled. He walked back into the kitchen, using his flannel sleeve to dust off what looked like a picture frame. He placed it in front of Tristan.

"Your wedding day," Tristan said.

"Your mom was so beautiful. We had no idea what trouble was coming our way, but I would do it all over again."

"Even though she left you?"

"On that altar, I promised to love her all my life, through sickness and in health. That's what I did. Those were the vows I took. It was hard. There were so many hard days."

Tristan patted his dad on the back. "You're a good man."

His dad nodded.

"As much as I love hearing you reminisce about Mom, I'd really like to know what you think about everything I've told you. This is a big life change. There's no going back."

His dad cleared his throat. "I don't know how any of this stuff works, but didn't you already make a commitment as a priest?"

Tristan nodded. "I will always be a priest, but my request to be dismissed from the clerical state was accepted."

His dad winced. "What does that mean?"

"Basically, I won't be able to perform any priestly duties anymore, but I will be able to get married within the Catholic Church."

"I've never heard about this."

"It's really rare. The Pope had to approve of my request."

"The Pope, as in Pope Francis?" His dad scratched his head. Tristan nodded. "You're on a first-name basis with him?"

Tristan laughed. "Not at all, but the Pope considered my situation and gave me dispensation from my vow of celibacy."

"Well, Tris, it's a lot to think about."

"You know, in the Eastern rites of the Catholic Church, married men can become priests."

"Eastern rites?"

"Yea, like Byzantine churches. They're every bit as Catholic as us Roman Catholics. They just practice their liturgy in a different way."

"Hmm." His dad nodded slowly. It was hard to tell what he was thinking.

Though in his thirties, Tristan still longed for his dad's approval. "Did you know Pope Adrian II was married and had a daughter?"

His dad shook his head. "Nope. Never even heard of Pope Adrian II."

Tristan huffed. "Dad, I came here for your support. I don't feel like I'm getting any from you."

"Well, maybe if you're feeling so torn about it, you shouldn't have done it."

Tristan pursed his lips. He wanted to slam his fist on the table. "I'm not torn about it. I just wanted some validation from my father."

"Do you think I wanted to stand by your mother all these years as she drank into oblivion?" He jabbed his finger at the wedding photo. "Do you think I wanted to resign myself to being alone until she died? Of course not, but I did it because I made a promise to love her until death, and that's what I did. Being a priest, I'm sure, isn't a walk in the park, but neither is being married."

Tristan rose from his chair. "You seem bitter, and maybe that's why you're having a hard time imagining me happy."

His dad started to weep and spoke in between sobs. "I just thought that after all you had been through, that you becoming a priest was the one thing I could point to and say that at least I didn't fail you in that way. You still had your faith." His dad stabbed his eye with his thumb, wiping away the tears. "I didn't want you to get married and suffer like I did. I was so relieved when you became a priest."

Tristan reached for his dad's wrinkled hands. "Not all marriages are like that."

"You're right. I loved your mother, but it wasn't easy. It wasn't a fairy tale. I just don't want you to run away from something because it's hard. You can't marry Violet and then decide in two years that you want to go back to being a priest. Whatever you choose, you need to commit to the love you vow."

"I will."

Chapter 28

It was a rare Saturday morning that Violet didn't have to work, but she tossed and turned in bed for a couple of hours before giving up just after 7 a.m. She stumbled out to the back porch and onto one of the rocking chairs. The gentle lull of the waves and a light breeze reminded her why she loved Maine. She hugged her legs into her chest.

Tristan didn't know it, but she had made up her mind and was ready to tell him.

"Vi, what are you doing up so early?" Sadie ducked her head out the porch door.

"I couldn't sleep."

"Join the club," Sadie said. "Want some coffee?"

"Actually, could you make me some tea? The mint one." It reminded her of Grandma.

Sadie returned a couple minutes later and handed a mug to Violet. She hugged her fingers around the warm cup.

"So what's your mind racing about this morning?"

Violet groaned. "Tristan."

Sadie nodded. "I figured. Did something happen?"

"No, nothing in particular. It's just a lot to take in. You know how I procrastinate on decisions."

"Aren't you guys just dating? What's to decide right now?"

Violet shrugged. "You're right. There's nothing urgent, but there's also no point in putting anything off, if I've already made up my mind."

"Have you?" Sadie asked. "Made up your mind?"

Violet bit her lip and nodded.

"Seriously? You guys have been on two dates."

"I know, but it's not like we're strangers. I know what I need to know about him."

Sadie took a sip of her coffee. "Mofo! This is hot, hot, hot!" She threw down her mug. "So, you're going to marry this guy, aren't you?"

Violet giggled and took a sip of her tea, buying time to decide what to say. "Time will tell." Why couldn't she just be honest with her sister that she in fact planned to end things with Tristan? Maybe she didn't want it to feel real. Maybe if she left Sadie guessing, then it meant she still had time to change her mind.

Sadie rolled her eyes. "Suit yourself. I never liked him, but if you insist that he's changed, then I'll take your word for it. You always have been the more mature of the two of us."

"Now you finally admit it!" Violet laughed. After they finished their drinks, Sadie left for the gym. Violet still had a few hours until she needed to leave for the cottage Tristan had rented for the weekend. He'd offered to pick her up so they could drive together, but she knew that after she gave him the letter she'd written, she would want to leave in her own car. Now that she was alone, she grabbed the white lined paper from her room and reread her letter. It had taken her a few hours to write, because of her dyslexia, but she knew how much Tristan appreciated letters. As she finished, she wiped a single tear from her eye.

* * * * *

The drive to the cabin seemed to take forever, probably because Violet knew what would come next. Should she break the news to Tristan first? Or after they ate? She felt guilty for letting him book the cabin when she knew she would be leaving shortly. As soon as she walked in and saw his smile, her heart sank. He had no idea. It crushed her to think that she'd be the reason for his tears. Yet, she still felt convicted that this is what she needed, and wanted, to do.

They hugged for a good minute and exchanged tales of their drives to the cabin. Violet wasn't sure how much longer she could engage in small talk. She had to come clean. She'd botched her attempt at honesty with Jude, and she wasn't going to do it again.

Violet cleared her throat and asked for some water.

Tristan rubbed her back. "Are you ok?" He grabbed a chilled bottle of water.

"Honestly, I don't feel great." Violet took a long gulp. "Thanks. Can we sit down?"

"Of course. Is there anything else I can get you?"

Violet shook her head and sat down on the fluffy, navy blue couch. It was soft and inviting, and she wished she could just fall asleep on it, instead of having this difficult conversation. "I'm all set." She took a deep breath, steadying her voice.

"Tristan…" She shook her head. "I can't continue in this relationship with you." She held her breath for a few seconds, waiting for Tristan to say something.

He nodded his head slowly. "Did something happen?"

Violet started to crumble. She avoided eye contact at first but knew he deserved her openness. "I wish I could say that there was a major turning point, or that you said or did something, but there's not. It's a decision I've come to through discernment and prayer, and lots of tears, as I'm sure you can see." She rubbed her wet eyes. What else could she say? Would anything lessen the blow?

His face was stoic. "Ok. I have to accept that."

Is that all he's going to say? "I'm so sorry. I never wanted to break your heart."

Tristan enveloped his hands in hers. "It's ok. I'm grateful that you gave me a second chance. I never thought we'd have this opportunity to fall in love again. You taught me that I could fall in love again."

"I hope you don't feel like you left the priesthood for nothing, now." Were there any tissues nearby? She opted to wipe her nose with her long shirtsleeve.

"Not at all, Vi. I made that choice without talking to you about it and without knowing whether you'd even want to see me again. As much as I love you, it wasn't about you, at the end of the day. If you and I were to get married, I would have loved that, but ultimately, I made the decision to leave the priesthood for myself."

Violet sniffled. "So you're not mad at me?"

Tristan shook his head. "Not at all. Am I sad? Yes. Does this hurt like crazy? Absolutely. But you're the mother of my two kids in heaven. We made saints together. You'll always have a special place in my heart." He kissed her hands in his, and she knew it'd be the last time.

Violet stood up from the couch and grabbed her purse. "Obviously, now it doesn't make sense for me to stay, but I wrote you a letter. It explains everything. I hope it can bring you comfort."

They hugged each other again and said goodbye. When Violet returned to her car, it felt like the floor had fallen out from under her. Her legs felt like jelly. *What have I done? Is it really over?* One heartbreak that year had been enough, but two felt like too much. Before pulling out, she knew she could run back inside into Tristan's arms and tell him that she wanted to spend the rest of her life with him. It was tempting, but she knew it was a momentary impulse that would pass. She reversed out of the driveway and drove home.

Chapter 29

Tristan couldn't bring himself to watch Violet pull out of the driveway. He stayed in the kitchen until he was certain she'd be out of sight. It felt like his legs would give out and he'd fall into a feeble heap on the floor at any moment. What was he going to do here all alone? What was he going to do in general with his life? Every time he thought of the future, he thought of Violet. She permeated his visions of family life: Saturday mornings in the fall at a cider mill, summers splashing in a pool, and Christmas mornings opening Santa's gifts. Would any woman fill that role now? He'd been certain that he and Violet were headed toward marriage. Had he totally misread her? He grabbed her note and sank into the couch.

Dear Tristan,

If I know you the way I think I do, I know you'll be replaying today's conversation over and over again. I just want you to have my thoughts in writing so you don't have to second-guess what I meant or why I'm doing this.

I'm crying as I write this. That's why some of these words are smudged. Seven years ago, I never thought I would see you again. You made it clear that you had no intention of ever committing to me, and in some ways, that finality was easier to accept than a gray area of maybe he will, maybe he won't.

But thinking I'd never see you again and never thinking of you again were two different things. I thought of the twins every day, so how could I not also think of you? It wasn't in a wishing way, but in a sentimental way.

I didn't realize how much anger I held onto until I ran into you at confession. It brought on pain that I didn't want to bear. I knew I still hadn't forgiven you, and you coming back into my life was, I think, a nudge from God to finally let go.

That's what I've done.

You've come into my life, and I learned to love you again. That bitterness that once suffocated my heart is gone. I firmly believe that God brought us together to mend both of our hearts and then let us part as fuller beings.

I know that sounds crazy because you feel like I've just broken your heart. I'm not walking away unscathed, either, but I finally have no more anger or resentment toward you. I hope you, too, can feel a sense of closure about our relationship. This goodbye felt like a long time coming.

I've loved these last few weeks together. I fell in love with you again. It felt like almost eight years ago when we first met, except this time I felt much more secure in your feelings for me. I wasn't wondering if you'd call back or ghost me. This time, I could count on you. It was an amazing feeling to be so cherished like that. Thank you.

The kind of man you are today is the kind I always knew was within you. You were so confused and wounded when we dated. It's a miracle we lasted as long as we did. The truth is, I don't want you out of my life, but at the same time, I know I can't have this life both ways. I can't marry someone else and still have a personal friendship with you. It's not fair to the man I marry.

And so, you may wonder: Am I leaving you for Jude? The answer is, not exactly. I still haven't spoken to him since we broke up, so I have no idea if a relationship with him is even an option. I intend to try to make amends with him. I don't know if he'll want to date me again, but the knowledge that it might not work out with him gives me confidence to say that this isn't about you versus another man.

There wasn't a moment or something you said that made me realize we had to part. There was no transgression. There was nothing you could have done differently, so I never want you to second-guess what happened between us. Please know that I've prayed and agonized over this. I know that it will give you little comfort, but I want you to know that I did not come to this lightly.

My grandpa always told me the Good Lord made our hearts capable of loving more than one person in our lifetime, in case we ever lost the love of our life and wanted to fall in love again. This past year, for the first time, I experienced my heart in love with two men at the same time. I think that's the beauty of this life—you must choose. I can only commit to one person.

Vi

P.S. Thank you for following through on your donation to the crisis pregnancy center.

By the end, a few of his tears smudged the blue ink. He wasn't wrong. She did love him. They loved each other, but she was choosing not to spend the rest of her life with him. His twins were gone, and now so was their mother. This time, it was for good.

Why, Lord? Why? Tristan punched the couch several times, grunting with the effort. *Was I not supposed to leave the priesthood? Was this your sign that I made the wrong choice again?* He felt tempted to say the Lord's name in vain, but held back.

He walked into the kitchen and opened the fridge. The sight of the strawberry ganache cake he'd brought for the two of them made his heart sink even further. He'd lost his appetite, but he took the cake out anyway for some comfort. It was a cake his mom made him growing up, one of the only things she could bake. She'd never taught him how to make it, so the closest he got to reliving it was from a bakery in downtown Portland. He had hoped to tell Violet more about his mom and highlight some of their good memories.

He turned on the TV for distraction. It was on the weather channel, showing the forecast for today, Saturday, July 1st. Wait. July 1st? In the frenzy of planning the weekend, he'd forgotten the calendar had jumped to July.

July 1st. *Happy birthday, Mom.*

Chapter 30

———•———

For Violet, her weekend at a cabin with Tristan had turned into a weekend of watching cheesy rom-coms with Sadie, who even volunteered to attend Mass with her on Sunday. Violet opted to take sick days on Monday and Tuesday. A broken heart counted as an illness, right?

Even though she was approaching her one-year anniversary at the station, she still worked on the morning show. Back at work on Wednesday, she wrapped up her day just after noon. Her only consolation for working these awful hours was summer afternoons of cloudless sunshine awaiting her at the end of her shifts. She checked her phone to make sure she and Jude were still scheduled to meet. She'd reached out to him the day before with a simple text, asking if she could talk to him.

It had been almost five months since they broke up. He could have a girlfriend for all she knew, but she wanted to set the record straight with him. Even if he never wanted to see her again, he should at least know the real reason she'd left was not solely because he'd kept the abortion from her.

When she pulled into his apartment complex, she went through the motions that had once been so familiar: press floor 5 on the elevator, get off, turn left, and walk four doors down. She knocked on the mahogany door. Would Jude hear her heart pounding when they hugged? Would they hug?

He opened the door, his brown shaggy hair tousled about and his eyes shining. His chocolate irises soothed her already.

"Hi," Violet said with a shy smile.

"Hey. Come in." Jude moved back to let her pass. "Can I get you something to drink?"

"I'd love some lemonade, if you have it." It was strange to be so formal with Jude. She wanted to leap into his arms and hug him.

"Sure do." He grabbed a jug of Arnold Palmer from the refrigerator and poured some into a glass.

"Thank you." She stood at his kitchen island and took a slow sip while she figured out how to explain everything. She clenched and relaxed her fists, and surveyed the room for any evidence of another woman. Any fruity scents? A bobby pin lying around? She reminded herself that it didn't matter. That's not why she was here. "I'm sorry that I walked out on you and our relationship when you opened up to me about the abortion. For years, I couldn't forgive myself and worried that people wouldn't accept me for my past, but then when you asked for my acceptance, I wouldn't give it to you."

The months apart made her feel like she'd lost some ground on being able to read him. What was going on in his head? She moved to the couch while Jude settled into a chair across from her. It was the same seating arrangement as when they had broken up.

He didn't look in any rush to speak up, so she continued. "I understand why you didn't tell me. My reaction confirmed your fears. The thing is, that same day, I wanted to tell you something, and I never did."

His eyes widened slightly, but he still maintained his poker face.

"I was already really mad at myself for what I'd done, and I figured that once I told you, you would dump me. So I used your confession as an easy way out, so to speak. I saved face."

"Ok." His forehead crinkled in confusion.

Am I really about to go through with this? "What I wanted to tell you was that Tristan and I got very close to kissing each other while you and I were still engaged. It was a one-off. I confessed it. I was going to tell you, but you mentioned the abortion first, and then I chickened out." Violet tried to decipher his poker face for any twitch of emotion. "I have no excuse for putting myself in that position. I couldn't understand why God let Tristan reappear in my life. I kept worrying it was some sort of sign that I was making a mistake with you, but now I realize that's not at all why he brought Tristan back into my life."

"Ok."

Violet inhaled four beats and exhaled. Jude wasn't rushing her, but he wasn't advancing the conversation either.

"The day after you and I broke up, I reached out to Tristan and told him I didn't want any more contact with him."

"So you two haven't been in touch since then?" Jude asked.

Not looking forward to explaining this part, either. "Actually, we have been in touch, which brings me to something else."

"I think I see where this is going," Jude said. "I heard he left the priesthood."

"Hear me out. I think you might be surprised." Jude bit his lip, but she could tell he tried to keep a cold demeanor.

She explained how Tristan asked her out after leaving the priesthood.

"I wondered if something was going on," Jude said. "I never suspected you two were together, but I figured he must've been wrestling with some sort of decision because there were rumblings at church about where he was and what he was doing."

"I can imagine. It's not something that happens every day."

"Your name never came up, though."

"Well, that's good. So, we went on a few dates, but in the end, I decided that God wasn't calling me to marry him. The thought of marrying him didn't bring me peace or excitement. I didn't want to spend the rest of my life with him. So, I walked away."

Jude looked even more confused now. "Wow, that must have been really hard."

"It was. He was crushed."

"I know what that feels like," he muttered.

Her heart sank. "I know." She lowered her head and exhaled. "I felt relieved after I told him. I realized that all along, he felt like my only connection to the twins. I had this fantasy that if he and I were together, we could just recreate what we'd lost, and I wouldn't feel pain anymore. But I don't think that's a basis for a marriage. I wasn't letting myself be really loved…by you. I sabotaged our relationship, and I'm sorry. I just wanted you to know. I don't want you to beat yourself up thinking that a mistake from your past is what ruined our relationship."

She had no idea what Jude would say or do. Would he laugh at her? Knowing him, that seemed improbable, but would apathy from him be worse? She assured herself that was unlikely, too.

Jude stood from his chair, came over to the couch, and sat next to her. Their legs brushed, but neither of them moved away. Warmth spread from her stomach at the familiar and thrilling contact. He put his arm around her, pulled her close, and inhaled deeply.

"I love you," he whispered into her ear.

"Really?" Her heart swelled. Jude nodded.

"I love you, too." She felt as if she woke from a nightmare to realize her terrors weren't real and that she was, in fact, safe. They intertwined their fingers.

"That felt too easy," she said. "Aren't you going to question or chastise me?"

"No, I'm not going to chastise you. Maybe, I'll have some questions, but I've done my own growing these last few months. I'm glad you explored a relationship with Tristan because I wouldn't have wanted you to marry me kicking and screaming down the aisle."

She laughed. "It wasn't like that, and you know it."

"I know. I just like giving you a hard time. I missed that."

"Me too."

Jude played with her fingers. "I was nervous about getting married, too."

"You were?"

"Yea, of course. It's a big commitment. Then, you hear about all of the people who get divorced, and you start to wonder if you're any different than they are."

"It's like writing a blank check."

He nodded and pulled her in tighter. "I missed you so much. So much."

"I missed you like crazy." His scent reminded her of home, and she felt sheltered in his arms. "How have you been? What's been happening in your life?"

"A whole lot of the same. I still go to work. I still eat, poop, and sleep every day." She laughed, relieved that he could still tease her. "In all seriousness, though, it's good. I was giving myself until the end of this month to reach out to you."

"Really?"

"I guess it was arbitrary, but I wanted to give it another shot. I had an inkling that you might give me another chance."

"You believed in us?" Violet asked.

"I talked to one of my sisters about it," he clarified. "She said that if it was her, that she'd be upset, too. She said all you needed to know was that I loved you and wanted to be with you. Actually, she predicted that you'd reach out to me. So I guess I owe her a hundred bucks now."

She elbowed him. "You guys bet on me?"

"It's for a good cause. She's going to donate it to the local food bank."

"What did your family think?"

Jude cringed. "They thought I was dumb for lying to you about Leona's abortion. None of them knew I hadn't told you. They were all surprised."

"I bet your mom had strong opinions about it."

"Oh, she did, but she was really compassionate, too," he said. "She thought about calling you to convince you to forgive me."

Violet gasped. "No, she didn't!"

"Yes, she did, but I told her not to. I didn't want you to feel pressured into anything. Like I said, I was planning to reach out to you anyway."

"Sure, sure," Violet teased. "I always felt welcomed by your family. I don't know if I appreciated that enough."

"They love you."

Violet reached for Jude's face, his stubble sprouting around his mouth. "I'm sorry."

"It's ok. I love you." The consolation of his words calmed her down. "So what's Father Tristan going to do now?"

"I'm not sure," she said. "I didn't ask, but I hope he finds what he's looking for. He'll be ok." She thought of how Sister Maria knew Father Goren would be ok when she broke up with him, and she knew the same was true for Tristan.

"We should pray for him," Jude said.

"I agree."

Jude tapped Violet on the thigh. "I'm hungry. Do you want to grab a bite?"

"Absolutely."

* * * * *

Violet and Jude finished the evening at their favorite gelato spot after lingering over a late lunch for three hours.

Violet savored another spoonful of her pistachio gelato. "By the way, did you and Leona know whether you were having a boy or a girl?"

Jude's face scrunched up. "That's random."

"You don't have to answer."

"No, it's fine. It just feels like it came out of nowhere. We're just eating gelato here."

She giggled. "Well, you know with me that I always have something going on between my ears."

"Very true." He took his time with another spoonful of his banana gelato. Violet cringed in disgust just thinking about the flavor. "We didn't know. It was too early in the pregnancy to find out."

Violet rubbed his back. She could tell he wanted to cry, but not in public. "It's ok."

"I still can't believe it happened. I still beat myself up. There wasn't only sadness but so much guilt, too."

"I wish I could relieve you from that burden." It felt like one of those moments where doing nothing but listening to the person in pain was the best choice. "Have you ever thought about going on a Rachel's Vineyard retreat?"

Jude shook his head. "What's that?"

"It's for people who lost children through abortion. I think it takes place over a long weekend. It's supposed to be really healing."

"Interesting. I'll think about it. Honestly, I don't know if I feel ready to forgive myself."

She frowned. "Why not?"

He exhaled. "I don't know."

"I don't want you to keep beating yourself up."

"You're one to talk. You're not exactly Mrs. Self-Compassion."

Violet protested. "I think I've grown in that department. You know what I've learned?"

Jude stole a spoonful of her gelato. "Tell me."

"Forgiving yourself is a daily task. I don't just forgive myself once and voila!" Violet snapped her fingers. "I might need to forgive myself every day and ask for God's help in that department because I don't think a day will ever go by where I don't think of the twins. In the same way, I want you to feel at peace with everything."

"Vi, in all seriousness, I appreciate it, but I'm a big boy, and I need to learn how to deal with my emotions."

She nodded. "Ok, I won't push you. I just want you to know it's possible to walk around and not feel the weight of that decision all the time." She dipped her spoon into Jude's cup and sampled a spoonful. She scrunched her nose and shook her head. "I don't know why I even tried. I hate that flavor."

"You're just so open-minded that you think you might like banana gelato one of these days. You've given it a lot of chances."

Violet kissed Jude on the cheek. "I'm just glad you gave me a second chance."

"Me too."

Epilogue

—————•—————

Violet and Jude relaxed on the porch of their hotel room overlooking the Mediterranean. It was the last full day of their honeymoon on the Greek island of Andros.

"I could never get tired of this view," she cuddled closer to Jude on the daybed and closed her eyes, committing to memory the crystal blue waters and the small white houses dotting the landscape across the bay. Jude's scent lingered between them, making her feel at peace. He kissed her forehead.

"We'll just have to come back," Jude started playing with her hair.

"I know we said no phones on the trip, but the photographer said she'd send some of the wedding photos while we're here. Do you mind if I check?"

"Go for it."

Violet leapt up and grabbed her phone from the back of a dresser drawer. She turned it on as she wiggled next to Jude again.

"I'm so excited!" Violet opened the email attachments from the photographer. "Oh, this one of Harper is so sweet!" She pointed to a picture of the seven-year-old skipping down the aisle with her tiny bouquet of lilies.

Jude laughed. "She took her role as the flower girl very seriously."

"She did! She practically ran down the aisle."

Jude kissed her nose. "She really looks up to you."

"I know. She's close to the same age as the twins would've been. After we broke up, it pained me to keep volunteering because she was such a reminder of the family I might never have."

"Now you don't have to worry."

Her heart dropped a beat. "Hopefully, we can get pregnant. I've always had this fear that I won't be able to conceive again."

"Did your doctors say anything about that?"

Violet shook her head. "It's just a fear I created, as if it's a punishment from God." Saying it out loud made her realize how silly it sounded.

Jude chuckled. "I don't think it works that way. And if we can't conceive, we'll adopt. We've talked about this. One way or another, we'll have a family."

Violet leaned forward and started kissing him more deeply, letting her phone fall off her lap. He squeezed her closer. *I love this man so much.* After a few minutes, she pulled away, out of breath. Jude blushed.

"Let's look at some more photos." Violet pointed to a photo of her mom walking her down the aisle. "Aww, I love this one."

She swiped to another photo of her and Jude walking out of the church at the end of the wedding Mass. They both beamed with huge smiles, eyes twinkling. "I definitely want to get that one framed for our bedroom."

After they scrolled through about a dozen more photos, Violet sighed. "I really don't want to go back to work the early morning shift and be a zombie again."

"You don't have to stay if you don't want to. You could take some time off and find something else you enjoy."

Violet clutched the Saint Pope John Paul II necklace Jude gave her on their wedding night. It included a pink lily charm to remember the twins. "I could do that, but it's just weird to think about a different career path. This is what I've done for almost ten years. I have a meeting with my boss in about two weeks, so maybe they're moving me up."

"Vi, you're so reliable, and the audience loves you in the morning. Is it possible that you've made yourself irreplaceable?"

"You have to say that because you're my husband now."

Jude laughed. "No, I'm serious. You have good chemistry with the whole morning team, and you have the kind of energy people want to see in the morning."

"So you're saying I'm not a hard-hitting journalist?" she lightly punched him in the rib.

Jude shook his head. "I'm giving you a compliment. You can do the hard-hitting stuff if you want to, but you have such a warm personality on air. That's why people love it when you cover the winter weather and the feel-good stories."

"I guess you're right. I think that's why I've been relegated to the morning show everywhere I've worked." She sighed. "Oh, well. I just don't think it's a good fit for when we have a family."

"We can cross that bridge when we get there, or you can leave before then. I'll support you in whatever you want to do."

"Thanks." Violet took Jude's hands in hers and kissed them. She rested her head on his chest. "I just want to savor our last day here."

Jude gently ran his fingers through her hair. "There is something I want to do when we go back home, though."

Violet piped up. "Oh? What's that?"

"I want to go on one of those Rachel's Vineyard retreats you told me about."

She stroked his chest. "That's great! I think you'll like it."

"I'm sure it'll be tough but also really healing."

"I promise you, it feels really good to forgive yourself."

Jude kissed her on the nose. "I believe you."

Someone tapped at their door. "I'll grab it," Jude said. Violet hadn't ordered anything, so she figured he was up to one of his generous shenanigans. He returned a minute later with a platter of chocolate-covered strawberries and two glasses of champagne, which he offered to her. "Cheers."

Jude took a gulp. "You're not having yours?"

"I don't want to risk it."

Jude's eyes bulged. "Vi, are you pregnant?"

"I could be and don't know it yet."

"Really?"

Violet rolled her eyes and giggled. "You do know how babies are made, right? We haven't been doing anything to avoid getting pregnant, and we have been on vacation for two weeks, so…who knows? Even if I was, it would be too soon for it to show up on a pregnancy test. We'll have to wait until we get back home."

"In that case, I will gladly drink your champagne and let you have my share of chocolate-covered strawberries."

"Sounds like a fair trade."

Jude picked a strawberry off the plate and popped it into Violet's mouth. Then, they settled back into each other's arms for one last night on their honeymoon.

CPSIA information can be obtained
at www.ICGtesting.com
Printed in the USA
LVHW010423110322
713215LV00002B/52

9 781737 541318